Trachea

a novel in linked stories

MAYANK BHATT

We acknowledge the support of the Canada Council for the Arts for our publishing program. We also acknowledge support from the Government of Ontario through the Ontario Arts Council, and the support of the Government of Canada through the Canada Book Fund.

Canada Council for the Arts Conseil des arts du Canada

Mawenzi House is a certified Benetech Global Certified Accessible™ (GCA) Publisher. The ebook version of this book meets GCA accessibility standards.

Cover art: Charles O'Rear / Bombay at Twilight / Getty Images
Cover design by Sabrina Pignataro

Library and Archives Canada Cataloguing in Publication

Title: Trachea : a novel in linked stories / Mayank Bhatt.

Names: Bhatt, Mayank, author.

Identifiers: Canadiana (print) 20250240114 | Canadiana (ebook) 20250240173 | ISBN 9781774151891 (softcover) | ISBN 9781774151914 (PDF) | ISBN 9781774151907 (EPUB)

Subjects: LCGFT: Novels.

Classification: LCC PS8603.H388 T73 2026 | DDC C813/.6—dc23

Printed and bound in Canada by Coach House Printing

Mawenzi House Publishers
192 Spadina Ave, Suite 417
Toronto, ON, M5T 2C2
Canada

www.mawenzihouse.com

CONTENTS

BOMBAY

Trachea

It was while rummaging through Ma's bag that I discovered a police postmortem report. Ma kept the bag in a cupboard close to her bed, neatly wrapped in red cloth. I had seen it many times before, because Ma was mostly under sedation or often in a daze, uncertain of her surroundings. The bag contained papers and old photographs about my Baba—they made me feel my Baba's presence. This time I discovered a new piece of paper in the bag. As I read it, my heart began to beat rapidly, and I felt a constriction in my throat and chest. I felt dizzy. I clutched the document and read it several times, but there wasn't much that I understood. Words like "trachea," "carotid artery," and "exsanguination" were unfamiliar to me; the Cause of Death section explained, "significant blood loss, leading to death."

The report was dated 20 September 1966. My Baba's name, Sadashiv Mahajan, was on the report that JJ Hospital had issued and a coroner had signed. I didn't know what or who a coroner was. Many years later, when I was a journalist, one day I met a coroner at the hospital morgue to report on a building collapse at Chimna Butcher Street that had killed thirty-two people.

I took the document from the bag, which I pushed back into the cupboard. Ma would look for it; she did so periodically, spreading the contents on the floor before carefully tying the red cloth over them and sliding the bag back into the cupboard. The bundle had a photo—now warped—of my parents on their wedding day, two silver coins, an image of Ganapati, some papers.

I took the document with me and kept it in the small wooden almirah that Dadi had allotted to Neeta and me to keep our clothes, books, toys, and everything else that we called ours. I folded the document and slid it between the pages of a large storybook that Aparna had gifted to Neeta and me. I wanted to show the document to Neeta.

I had heard the word "suicide" before, uttered in hushed whispers. I didn't know what it meant. But from the looks on the faces of the people who came to meet my grandmother and my mother after the funeral, it was obvious that it meant something bad. While Dadi met the visitors with infinite patience and fortitude, Ma refused to meet anyone.

I remember the day vividly, when in the afternoon our neighbour Sadanand Kaka came to my school. I was surprised to see him. The school principal—the stern-looking Joshi Sir—brought him to the class.

In those days, our family occupied the entire second floor of the building; Baba had rented the extra room on the other side of the stairwell to Aparna, a young colleague who had come from Aurangabad. Sadanand Kaka and his wife Radha Kaku were on the first floor.

"We have to go home, Sharad," Sadanand Kaka said. I could make out that something was not right. Neeta was already with him, clutching his forefinger. He led us both out of the school, and we sat in a taxi that was waiting at the school gate.

"What happened, Kaka?" I asked.

"You have to come to my home today," he said, but he didn't look at me.

"What happened, Kaka?" I asked again.

"Your father is not well. The doctors are looking after him. Neeta and you have to be with us today," he said.

I saw an ambulance standing near our building. Radha Kaku came to the taxi and the couple hurriedly took Neeta and me up the stairs to the first floor. They quickly closed the door behind them. Neeta went and sat on the jhula that was there, looking pensive.

"What happened?" she asked Radha Kaku.

"Baba is not well. Your Dadi told us to get both of you from school and keep you here," Radha Kaku said.

"Sadanand Kaka, what happened to my Baba?" I asked. "Why aren't you telling me?"

"Sharad, your father is injured. The doctor is here from the hospital. Your Baba will be taken there. Your grandmother and your mother will have to go with him," he said.

I couldn't stop my tears. Neeta got off the jhula and came to me.

"Don't cry, everything will be all right," she said. My six-year-old sister was consoling me; I was all of eleven years.

Sadanand Kaka went upstairs to our home, leaving Neeta and me with Radha Kaku. She poured warm milk mixed with turmeric into two cups and handed them to us. I took mine even though I hated milk. I sat on the couch near the window so that I could see the ambulance below. After I had finished the milk, I saw four men carry a stretcher covered in white cloth; Sadanand Kaka was one of the men, the others were from our neighbourhood. Dadi walked down behind them. I didn't see Ma.

Radha Kaku and Neeta joined me at the window. The ambulance drove away and the crowd that had gathered dispersed.

"What is happening?" It was now Neeta's turn to ask. I instantly realized, when I saw the stretcher, that there was a body beneath the white cloth, and it was our Baba.

"Baba is dead," I said. My throat had dried, and my voice was hoarse.

Radha Kaku clutched both of us and began to bawl loudly when Sadanand Kaka returned. He looked annoyed but restrained himself. "The kids will be with us today. There is a lot of cleaning up to be done upstairs," he said.

"Nobody accompanied the body?" Radha Kaku asked.

"No, the police will be involved, there will be a postmortem. So the cremation will be later."

"Where is she?" Radha Kaku asked.

"She has gone to her Masi's home in Parel. The house is a mess. There is blood all over—" He stopped when he saw Neeta and me staring at him.

"How did Baba die?" I asked, looking at Sadanand Kaka. Neeta had gone back to the swing.

"He got injured," he said.

"So, he is dead," I said. But he didn't look at me.

"When do we go home? I want to be with Ma," I said.

"Yes, I want to go home!" Neeta shouted from the jhula.

"I will take you home in the evening," Sadanand Kaka said.

But sometime later, to our relief, Dadi came to get us. "They can come home now; their presence will help their mother. I have cleaned the room, and except for a few stains on the wall near the door, there are no traces." She spoke in a firm, cold, matter-of-fact tone that didn't betray any emotion.

Even now, when I recall the day, the thing that I remember most is my Dadi's steely determination, her willpower and self-restraint. As she climbed the stairs with us, she held our hands gently. When we reached the second floor, she knelt and hugged us tightly.

"You be with Ma. She needs you. Don't ask her any questions. Don't talk to her. Just be with her," she whispered.

I hadn't seen Ma the way I found her that afternoon. She looked at us and then looked out of the window. Dadi made us sit next to her on the bed. We looked at Ma in bewilderment, unsure of what to do. Ma was crying softly. She held our hands and lightly hugged Neeta.

"Do whatever your Dadi tells you to do. Look after your sister. And don't become like your Baba," she said to me.

Then she began to laugh, looking grotesque because she was still crying. Dadi came to her and said, "Your children need you more than ever before." Her voice quavered. She was a mix of concern and anger. She walked away into the kitchen.

Ma looked at Dadi and wanted to say something but restrained herself. She got up from the bed and went to the kitchen, poured water into a steel mug and gulped it down. She looked at herself in the mirror, tried to pat her hair into place; wiped away her tears, and returned to her bed.

Neeta climbed onto the bed and put her head on Ma's lap, but Ma pushed her away. Neeta looked at me in disbelief and began to whimper. I led her away to the window and made her sit on Dadi's chair. She hugged me. "Don't cry now, please, or she will get angry," I whispered. She nodded.

I walked to the kitchen and saw Dadi sitting on the floor, clutching her head in her hands. She had an open bag and papers strewn on the floor. She looked up at me and beckoned me to come to her.

"Help me look for a bank passbook," she said. I sifted the papers in the bag, pulled the passbook out and handed it to her.

"Your mother is not stable, and I don't think she will ever be,"

Dadi said in a flat tone. "You have to take care of your sister and yourself if something happens to me."

"How did Baba die?" I asked.

"Your mother—" she began, then stopped herself, then said, "He slit his throat."

I gasped and gaped at her; she pulled me to her and hugged me.

"Why did he do that, Dadi?"

"You are too young to understand; when you are older, you will, perhaps."

A moment later, Ma stormed into the kitchen and shrieked, "He died because he was not happy with us. He wanted to be with that *randi*!"

"Prameela, you stop this right now. They are your children!" Dadi shouted. I had not seen my grandmother this angry before.

Ma stormed out, muttering, "*randi*."

"You take Neeta downstairs to Sadanand's house, your mother is not well," Dadi said. "And then come right back up. We have to get some of your Baba's things from Aparna's house."

When I returned, Dadi led me to Aparna's flat across the stairwell. The flat was just two rooms, like ours—a living room and a kitchen. The rooms were sparsely furnished—just one steel cupboard, a wooden work desk, two chairs and a bed in the living room, and another spice shelf in the kitchen.

The living room had been mopped. I asked Dadi about it, and she said she herself had cleaned the room.

"I am still not done," she said and pointed at the spots on the floor, with footprints showing where the blood had not dried.

She began to mop the floor vigorously to clean the bloodstains.

"Sharad, look through the cupboard and the table and search for anything that is your Baba's," she said.

I opened the cupboard. Everything was artfully arranged. Nothing seemed out of place. But it was full of Aparna's clothes. In the safe inside the cupboard, which was unlocked, I saw some jewellery boxes and some documents. I pulled out the documents—papers that had been clipped together. I handed them to Dadi.

Dadi, who had learned the rudiments of English, read aloud: "The Last Will and Testament . . . " She folded the documents and handed them back to me.

"Go, keep this in my kitchen cupboard. Don't tell your Ma and come back at once and continue searching."

I scampered off and returned and continued to rummage through the cupboard but found nothing about my Baba. Then I began to rummage through the worktable. It had a file with electricity and cooking gas bills, a box of carbon paper, a box containing whitener, an eraser, pencils, and a ballpoint pen, and a folder with the lease agreement between Aparna and Baba. The table was clean, without a layer of dust. I picked up the eraser. It was the expensive variety that some of my classmates had at school, green on the top and white below, with a sweet smell. I put it in my trouser pocket. I took the lease agreement to Dadi, who again stopped mopping and checked the document.

"Oh good," she exclaimed. "She has to leave next month."

Dadi finished mopping the floor, which was now clean without a trace of blood, but there were a few stains on the wall near the bed and I pointed them out to her. She handed me a piece of cloth.

"Rub them hard and see if they come off," she said.

While I was wiping, I mustered enough nerve to ask her, "Tell me, Dadi, what happened?"

"He must have slit his throat with a shaving blade. Many times," she said. She displayed no emotion. Her voice was steady. She looked at me without feeling sorry for herself or for me.

But I began to whimper. “Why did he do that?” I asked.

“God knows. I suppose he could not face the reality,” she said. She walked to the bed and sat on it. She told me to stop cleaning and come sit beside her. When I obeyed, she hugged me, heaved, and convulsed before letting out a muffled scream. I hadn’t heard anyone cry so softly and yet so hard.

Dadi wasn’t interested in following any rituals. After the postmortem was done and the hospital had released the body, she took Sadanand Kaka and me to accompany it in a hearse to the crematorium, where, after performing a few rituals under the guidance of a priest, I lit the pyre and consigned Baba’s body to the flames. The crematorium attendant gave us some bones from the pyre, which we collected in a plastic jar. Sadanand Kaka hailed a taxi and we drove to Banganga to immerse the bones in the pond there.

Not too many of my family’s relatives or friends came to visit us following Baba’s death. This was perhaps due to the circumstances. The man had killed himself in the home of a young woman, who was a neighbour, when his family—his wife, children, and mother—were in the house next door. The neighbours were helpful because they had all known what was going on between my father and Aparna, and they would have probably told Dadi or Ma about it, and I am assuming that both these women did not respond appropriately to the situation as it unfolded.

Fortunately, Aparna decided to leave. She came home late one evening. Neeta was already asleep, and I was doing my homework before going to bed. Dadi knocked, opened the door, and Aparna gave her the keys. No words were exchanged. Ma came briefly out into the corridor, saw Aparna, and, muttering abuses, returned to the living room.

Dadi told me to follow Aparna and see what she was taking. I saw a man in Aparna's flat helping her put her things into three large metal trunks. She smiled when she saw me.

"It is late for you to be awake," she said.

I didn't respond and looked at the bags.

"Don't worry, I will only take what is mine," she said.

"Aparna, be quiet. Let's get the packing done and get out of here," the man said sternly.

Together, they packed the trunks and left in a taxi. Dadi came to inspect the apartment and checked everything, opening the cupboard, looking under the bed, opening the drawers of the worktable. When she was satisfied, she patted me on the back. "You are a good kid," she said, and smiled.

I wasn't sure I deserved that accolade. I had just stood and watched them pack.

"Who was that man with her?" I asked. I couldn't think of anything else to say.

"Her brother. She will be with her brother's family."

"Who will come here?"

"We will have to see. Someone who can pay good rent. Ghanshyam, the *sabziwala*, wants to move in. He got married last year and now his wife is arriving from their village."

Ghanshyam and his wife moved into the apartment in a week.

Ma was no longer the person she was before. She had always had a weak constitution. She would tire easily, fall ill often, need to rest in the middle of a chore. But she was always attentive to everyone's needs. Now she seemed lifeless, without energy even to look after herself. The deterioration in her health—both physical and mental—became obvious after Baba's suicide, but it had started earlier.

Dadi said it had to do with Aparna. In the absence of any other obvious reason, I believed what she said. I have no recollection of any tension or quarrels between my parents. We didn't go out much because we couldn't afford to. Baba was an accountant in a paint company that had been nationalized; its owners had stripped it of all its assets and left it to die. From being on the verge of unemployment, Baba had suddenly become a government employee, and everyone in the family was immensely proud of his new status. Ma had been giving tuitions to high school students even before she was married and continued to do so until Neeta was born. After Baba's suicide, she stopped the tuitions.

The house in which our family lived belonged to Dadi. My grandfather had left it for her in his will. The building, which was in Teli Gali, had two spare rooms, and Dadi, being pragmatic, had rented them out. She continued to complain about my Dada's lack of resourcefulness many years after he had passed away.

In those days, houses were let out on what were known as "leave and license" agreements, which were renewable annually. Ever since I could remember, our neighbours were tenants who moved in temporarily, and because of that they were usually single men who had recently arrived, looking for a job.

After a particularly terrible experience with one of the male tenants, who would yell in a drunken stupor all night, Dadi decided that she would only have women tenants. That is when Aparna moved in. She was from Aurangabad and had joined the paint company as an administration clerk.

Many years later, when I asked my Dadi about Aparna, she told me that the woman was a friendly sort of person, who mixed easily with everyone. She was especially friendly with Baba. They went to work together, were together at work all day, returned from work together, and then Aparna would spend the evening with us. Dadi and Aparna also became friends, and she would often be in our kitchen, trying different recipes.

Dadi said Ma instinctively knew something was amiss and kept her distance from Aparna. She found Aparna's closeness to her husband irritating, and her annoyance transformed into all-consuming anger.

Dadi didn't tell me everything she knew in order to shield me from the foul gossip that spread after Baba committed suicide. But I think even she didn't know the complete story. I don't remember the exact period, but I think Aparna was our neighbour for some five years, and during this time, Ma became increasingly ill, often bedridden, and always distraught.

After Baba's suicide, Ma gave up doing household chores. The burden of supporting the family and the home fell squarely upon my Dadi. In an attempt to make Ma move on in life, Dadi tried to involve her in different activities, but she remained resolutely disinterested. Dadi suggested that Ma should perform the daily pooja at home, but Ma flatly refused.

"There is no *bhagwan*. And all this pooja is a waste of time," she declared.

"Hush, my dear. You shouldn't talk like that," Dadi said softly.

"If there was a *bhagwan*, I would not have seen what I saw," Ma said.

"Prameela, the kids are present . . . control yourself," Dadi said.

"They didn't stop," Ma shouted, her eyes blazing.

"Prameela, you won't say a word more," Dadi said, and walked up to Ma, held her in a tight hug, and led her to her bed.

That evening Ma had high fever and had to be taken to the hospital. She was sedated and returned only after a week. From then on, she was almost permanently kept under sedation.

Lemon

"Is it a kiss if I suck the lemon that you sucked too?"

Masuma looked at me but didn't answer. She smiled. She took the lemon back from me and sucked it again. Her lips puckered at the sour taste, and she shut her eyes, savouring the moment. Before giving it back to me, she sprinkled some more salt-pepper-and chilli powder on it. I sucked the lemon again, hoping to get a taste of her, but it just tasted tangy.

We had walked away from the others in our group, leaving behind the manicured lawns of the park, and into the wild growth of shrubbery. The forest and mountain were not too far. The heat from the early afternoon sun was intense; bees and other insects swarmed over our heads. Our palms were moist with sweat, our fingers intertwined into a firm grip, proclaiming our defiance, our daring, as it were, but there was no one around to be shocked at the sight of two teenagers walking in a park, holding hands, sucking a lemon.

We sat under a tree, still holding hands, and but for the buzzing of the insects and the chirping of the sparrows, it was all quiet.

I just wanted to be with her. There was nothing to say. She was quiet too; and that was odd because usually she just couldn't stop talking. Her loose glasses often slipped, and she pushed them impatiently up the bridge of her nose.

After a heartbreakingly long silence, which both of us couldn't bear but didn't know how to end, she asked: "Do you know the saddest short story in the world?" Without waiting for me to respond, she began narrating it.

"Once upon a time there was a couple, a woman and a man. They had been together for many years. Then one day the woman got sick and bedridden. The man looked after her for some time but then got tired and fell in love with another woman. He started giving his wife poison pills that would kill her gradually. The woman, who still loved her husband, knew that she was a burden on him. She would throw away the pills after the husband left the room. You see, she didn't want to live anymore, and she thought that if she stopped taking those pills, she would die sooner."

She paused and looked straight into my eyes.

"Men are such beasts," she declared, looking at me sternly.

I nodded agreeably, although I wasn't convinced that men were beasts. I mean, they could be, or they couldn't be. I wasn't one, for sure.

"I hope you don't grow up to be a beast," she said, looking at me accusingly. She seemed convinced that I would grow up to be one by default.

"Do you want to kiss me?" Masuma asked suddenly. We were still holding hands. She moved closer to me.

"I have never kissed a girl," I said, and I looked at her uneasily.

"Have you kissed a boy?" she asked, and smiled wickedly.

"No . . . "

"Okay, let me teach you how to," she said. She took off her glasses, pulled me closer to her, and put her lips on mine. She tasted of lemon. Then she pulled away. Her eyes were still shut tight.

"How was it?"

"Great! Open your eyes," I said. She did and smiled. "Did you like it?" I asked.

"You will get better with experience," she said.

"You will let me kiss you again?"

"Not today. We must go, or the others will come looking for us," she said, and got up and began to run. I followed her. We were the last pair to reach the class meeting spot. All the girls, including Masuma, giggled. We got on the school bus and returned to school.

I hadn't learnt anything new about plants and animals. But I had kissed a girl for the first time in my life. I was still in a bit of a daze. It was unbelievable. I had been with the most beautiful girl in our school, I was talking to her, walking with her, holding her hand, sharing a lemon with her, and kissing her, and the best part was that she was leading me all the way.

Mrs Iyengar taught us English. She was as tall as most of the class, which made her shorter than most adults. She wore a starched cotton sari every day and poured a bucket of coconut oil on her hair every morning. She also wore large, thick-framed glasses that she took off when she read. She knew she wasn't a favourite of her students and worked hard to uphold that reputation.

The first time I met Mrs Iyengar was on my first day at school in grade 10. She told me to sit in the second row in front of her. Masuma was sitting on the bench and moved a little to make place for me.

Mrs Iyengar was to be our class teacher. "If you don't know yet, let me inform you before we begin," she announced, and the class fell into a hushed silence.

"Our Prime Minister has declared a national emergency. She

has jailed all prominent leaders. Democracy is dead in India," Mrs Iyengar declared. We looked at her with bemused expressions. Then she placed a big book and a small book on her desk. She lifted the big book with some effort and held it up for all to see. It was bound in dark green cloth, with the spine and edges in deep brown leather. "This is the *Complete Works of Shakespeare*," she said, and then asked, "Who was Shakespeare?"

A number of hands went up, including Masuma's. Mrs Iyengar picked Masuma to answer.

"He was a writer. He wrote many plays," Masuma said in her tinny voice.

"Correct. Very good, Masuma," Mrs Iyengar said, and smiled at her. "Writers who write plays are called playwrights," the teacher added.

Then she lifted the smaller book and read aloud the title. "Lamb's *Tales from Shakespeare*. Shakespeare was a playwright. Plays are like the movies but instead of seeing everything on a big screen, there are live actors on a stage," Mrs Iyengar said. "How many of you have seen a play on a stage?"

Again, many hands went up, including Masuma's. But this time, Mrs Iyengar didn't pick her. She looked at me.

"I went to see a play in Gujarati with my Ma and Dadi," I lied. Had she asked me the name of the play, I would have been caught. I had never seen a play. But I didn't want everyone to know that we were poor. I looked at Masuma as I sat down. I nodded and smiled weakly.

"I am Sharad."

"I am Masuma. I am a new student," she said.

I offered her my hand, but she didn't want to shake it, so I let it fall limply on my lap.

In the background, Mrs Iyengar was talking about Shakespeare. I wasn't as interested in what she was saying as much as I was in this new girl sharing my bench. But she was listening with rapt attention to Mrs Iyengar's stentorian voice as she explained the importance of Shakespeare to the English language.

"After the Bible, Shakespeare has given the English language the most number of words, but if you read his original plays, you will not understand anything, which is why we read Lamb's version," Mrs Iyengar said.

Masuma came early to school and was among the first to arrive in the classroom. She carried two lunchboxes—one for the recess, like the rest of us, and one for before Mrs Iyengar took attendance. She would offer me whatever she had and watch me eat with a smile. Then she would open her workbook and write the date on a fresh page. The first page of her workbook had what appeared to be the letters *LAY*.

"What does that mean?" I asked, pointing at those letters.

"These are Arabic numerals for 786. They are holy numbers for Muslims," she said.

I nodded. I asked her if she had seen the latest Amitabh Bachchan film. Her eyes brightened and she smiled.

"I love movies, I see one every week at Ambar-Oscar," she said, referring to the only multiplex near our school. Bombay, being the centre of cinema, had three multiplexes as early as the 1960s; of course they weren't called multiplexes in those days.

"I would do that, too, but I am not allowed," I said. She could sense the envy in my voice and offered me another mawa cake.

"Pay attention," Mrs Iyengar bellowed, breaking the magical spell between us, and we looked up abruptly.

In a few days we became close friends. Boys in the class teased me about her. I told her about it, and she said some girls teased her, too.

"Ignore them," she said.

After a few days of feeling awkward about the derisive attention, we ignored the teasing. We were happy to be with each other. Every day, she spoke about her home. Her mom, her dad, her brother Sultan; it meant emperor, she said. I told her about my mom, my sister and my Dadi—my grandmother.

"What about your dad?" she asked.

"He passed away when I was young."

"You are still young," Masuma said, and hugged me. I gasped in surprise. Mrs Iyengar, who was engrossed in describing the balcony scene from *Romeo and Juliet*, stopped speaking and stared at us.

"Why are you hugging him, Masuma? Is Sharad feeling cold, or do we have our own Romeo and Juliet in our classroom?" she asked, glaring at Masuma and then at me. The classroom broke out into titters.

Masuma looked at the open book in front of her and pretended to read with rapt attention while trying hard to suppress a giggle. I was too dazed by her hug, and by Mrs Iyengar's stinging barb and the high-pitched laughter that filled the classroom. Tears welled up and began to flow down my cheeks. Masuma reached out to me and held my hand beneath the desk.

I was trudging down the school's compound later that day, still trying to comprehend Masuma's sudden show of affection, when I heard her calling out my name and turned to see her come running after me.

"Will you walk home with me?" She began walking with me even before I agreed. She offered me a piece of the pink chewing gum sold outside our school, which I had never tasted.

"I am not allowed to chew gum," I told her.

"Why not?"

"I wear partial dentures," I said.

"This is so weird, a kid with false teeth," she said, and laughed, but at once stopped when she saw I was annoyed. We walked quietly and reached the gate of Fidai Baug, the housing complex where she lived. A tall, burly boy, older than us, walked up to Masuma.

"Sultan, this is my classmate Sharad. He wears false teeth," she said.

Sultan looked at me and narrowed his eyes as he took the bag from Masuma. They walked inside through the arched door of the complex. Masuma smiled and waved goodbye. I renewed my trudge. When I was about to reach home, I saw Sultan come running after me. I stopped as he reached me, panting.

"Don't walk with my sister," he said, grabbing my shirt collar.

"She asked me to," I said; my voice came out thin, and I struggled to get out of his grip.

"Don't you ever walk with her near our home, even if she asks you to," he said menacingly, before letting go of me.

The next day, Mrs Murthy was teaching history—medieval Indian history where the kings battled each other all the time over some fort somewhere. She was strict and stern and not given to cracking jokes. She would rather crack a whip.

After my frightening encounter with Sultan, I resolved not to talk to Masuma. I didn't smile back when she smiled at me. I kept my school bag between us. After a few weeks she turned to me in exasperation, saying sharply, "What's the matter?"

"Your brother doesn't like me talking to you."

"Ignore Sultan. He is crazy," she whispered. She again reached out to me and held my hand. I tried to push her hand away, but she held on firmly. This time, I felt the softness of her palm. She patted me and smiled.

"Sharad, my brother is like all brothers," she said.

"Huh? What does that mean?" I asked.

She giggled and put my school bag on the floor. Then she moved closer to me. She continued to hold my hand and gently squeezed it. Nalini, who sat behind us, was peering over our shoulders to see what we were doing. Masuma looked at her and they both giggled.

Mrs Murthy, disturbed by the noise, looked at me in anger and disgust.

"OUT! Both of you, out of my class, right now," she hollered.

"I didn't do anything," I said, but she couldn't hear me.

"He didn't do anything," Masuma said.

"OUT! Out of my class, right this moment," Mrs Murthy shouted.

"Serves you right," Nalini whispered. I turned round in anger, but Masuma giggled again. She got up and I followed her out, ashamed of my humiliation.

We stood outside the classroom till the bell rang and then went down to the canteen to have the usal pav. She watched me intently as I dipped the pav into the usal and began to eat.

"Why are you staring at me?"

"Does it hurt?"

"What?"

"Does it hurt to chew with false teeth?"

"No, and they are called partial dentures," I said, irritated. "I have been wearing them since I was ten."

"Are you upset?"

"Everyone asks me about my dentures. It is like I am some sort of a human freak in a circus. My teeth didn't grow after my milk teeth fell off, because of all the medicines they gave me when I was an infant. I had pneumonia and my kidneys were swollen when I was just six months old," I said, breathing heavily.

She wanted to know more.

"I didn't want them but there was nothing I could do. I am the only kid in the whole wide world to have dentures."

I didn't realize it but tears were streaming down my face. Masuma got up and came over to my side of the table. She gently nudged me to move over and sat beside me. She held my hand again and pulled it to her lips and kissed it. I pulled my hand away. "Masuma, stop doing that. Everyone is looking," I whispered. She seemed oblivious to everyone's presence.

"You cry so easily," she said.

Masuma became the best thing to have happened to me. I had never had so much fun in school, and for that matter anywhere else. At home, Ma was battling her inner demons and was in a world different from ours. Neeta, my sister, was busy with her dolls and her playhouse.

My Dadi knew instinctively that something was up with me.

"Who is she, Sharad?"

"Who? What?"

"You are very pleased with yourself these days, very happy. Nothing at home has changed, so it must be at school. And you are sixteen, so it must be some girl. Who is she?"

"What?" I asked again, pretending not to have heard her.

She smirked but didn't say anything.

I hadn't mustered enough courage to walk with Masuma again after school. Sultan could well be on the prowl. But I reached school early just so that I could be with her for a little longer before Mrs Iyengar arrived in the class. Masuma always ate before the class commenced and always shared her food with me. Without quite realizing what I was doing, I was eating lamb and chicken. I only realized this when Mrs Iyengar asked all those who were vegetarians to raise their hands. I raised mine and Masuma pulled it down.

"You are not a vegetarian. You eat meat," she said.

"No, I don't."

"Yes, you do. You have been having my food. And you love it," she said, and laughed.

It was true. I loved the food she gave me.

One morning Masuma announced that we should bunk school again and go to the Juhu beach together, just the two of us. Without waiting for my response, she instructed me to sneak out of the classroom just after Mrs Iyengar had taken attendance, on the pretext of wanting to go to the washroom. She would follow later. We would return before the last class to collect our bags and then go home. I should wait at the bus stop, she instructed, and together we would take a bus to Juhu.

She had planned everything meticulously, and we reached Juhu beach in half an hour. We had bhel puri and falooda at the food stalls and then we took off our shoes and walked in the water, holding hands, the waves soaking us to our skin. Then she took me to the farthest end, where the beach ended in a thick foliage of trees and bushes. I had never been here before. She was clinging to me and shivering. We reached the bushes and I saw that there were many couples there kissing and groping. Nobody noticed anyone else, everybody busy doing their own thing.

Masuma found a place for us to sit and, still clinging to me, she pulled me down. A tree root tore my trousers and bruised my knee a bit and it began to bleed. She looked at the bruise and told me to off take my trousers. I wasn't sure I wanted to do that, but she deftly unbuttoned the trousers and pulled them down. She licked my bruised knee. My groin stiffened.

She pulled her shirt over her shoulders and unstrapped her bra. She moved over me. I pushed my face into her breasts. She smelled of talcum powder. I was fumbling but she was patient. She had her eyes shut tight and was kissing me when suddenly I saw someone grab her by her hair and pull her up. Sultan slapped her hard and pulled her shirt back in place. She was terrified and began to whimper. Then Sultan looked at me and was about to hit me when Masuma screamed: "If you touch him, I will kill myself."

Surprisingly, Sultan just pulled her by her hair and dragged her away.

Masuma didn't return to school. Mrs Iyengar called me to the teachers' common room one day and told me that Masuma's parents had informed her what Sultan had seen us doing at the beach, but they didn't want anyone in the school to know. They had decided to send Masuma away to Indore. My Dadi was called to school and was told about what I had done.

"I have failed," she muttered.

Later Nalini told me that Masuma's parents had got her married to an older man. I failed my 10th grade and began working at my uncle's office doing menial work.

I saw Masuma many years later, when I was on my way to Ambar-Oscar to see a rerun of *Jaws* with my cousin. She was wearing a hijab and holding a baby in her arms. A toddler was walking ahead of her. Masuma was talking to someone who I assumed was her husband. He looked distinguished and older. They seemed happy together.

We looked at each other and smiled. We moved on.

I haven't seen her since.

Fight

After school, I joined a college close to home, with the intention of finding a job later. Our family's financial situation was precarious and Dadi was keen for me to do some part-time work to manage my own needs at least. So I was made to join morning college and began to look for work.

That task turned out to be quite easy. Sadanand Kaka introduced me to Rajubhai, a contractor who supplied extras to film studios nearby. Our home was on a road leading to four studios.

"He always needs extras," Sadanand Kaka said, and promptly gave me a telephone number to call Rajubhai's office. We had two telephones in our neighbourhood—one was with Dr Mankodi and the other was at Ganesh Store. The doctor wouldn't let anyone use his phone. Ganesh Store charged 50 paise. I walked to the store and called Rajubhai. He called me right away to Mohan Studio. I got on a bus and reached the studio.

Rajubhai looked at me, observed me minutely for some time, then made some mental calculations and nodded.

"It is good that you are not fair-skinned. We need dark-skinned people to be the villains' sidekicks; you are not tall, but we will have to make do."

"What do I have to do?"

"Nothing. Just stand next to the actor and try to look mean."

"Who is the actor?"

"Kadar Khan, and the film is *Desh Premee*. Amitabh Bachchan is the hero, but you won't be anywhere near him, at least for now," Rajubhai said, anticipating and answering all my questions. "And yes, you will be paid fifteen rupees for every day you work."

This seemed like a good deal. "But what about lunch?"

He looked at me in annoyance, but then said, "Okay. You will have lunch with me and Monali at my office, but don't tell the others. Sadanand is a dear friend."

That day for four hours I stood next to an actor, doing nothing but looking mean. It was the most boring work I could imagine. I didn't have a choice. I would reach the studio after college and be there till the late evening. It was as full-time as it could get. After a week, Rajubhai told me I should work at his small office. "I need someone to manage all the paperwork, go to the bank, get all the permissions for shooting outdoors—it is becoming a big thing these days, shooting outdoors. Monali does that work, you help her."

I was delighted. This seemed easier than standing around doing nothing; and being on my feet all day was tiring.

Monali was Rajubhai's daughter. She was older than me by about five or six years. In fact, Rajubhai didn't want her to work at his office, he wanted her to get married and settle down.

"That is what women do," he said loudly during one of their arguments. But Monali shouted back that she didn't want to marry "a stranger chosen by my parents."

These arguments were frequent and conducted at any time of the day and in the presence of whoever was around. The father-daughter duo had no notion of privacy.

The office was at some distance from the studio, and nearer home, so I didn't have to take the bus. I walked from college to home and from home to the office every day. The office was a standalone structure with an asbestos roof and tin walls. But it was spacious, and it had two big fans that made even the melting Bombay summers somehow bearable.

Monali came around noon, when Rajubhai also reached the office for his lunch. He would take a cursory look at the paperwork and periodically nod. Apparently Monali was a good manager. She worked till evening. My job was to assist her. Initially she only assigned menial tasks to me. I was no more than a standby helper, but gradually my responsibilities grew.

A few days after I began work at the office, she introduced me to Jagan, whom I already knew. Jagan Bendre lived in Teli Gali with his family. He had a steady job as an accountant in a big textile manufacturing company that had an office in Ballard Pier. He was the only one from our neighbourhood who took the train to work every day from Andheri to Churchgate. Jagan was also involved with his company's trade union. He worked with Dhinmant Desai, an up-and-coming trade union leader, to organize the workers and get them a better deal.

"He is the reason I don't want to marry someone my parents choose," Monali said, looking at Jagan with unrestrained admiration, and then smiled at me.

Jagan smiled at her and then looked at me. He had a day off and had come to meet Monali. He had brought a vada-pav, which he gave to her, who handed it to me.

"Here, you have it," she said.

"No. I have had my lunch already," I said. I stood there looking at both of them, and felt happy for no reason. They looked good together.

"You have to help us," Monali said. "We want to get married."

I was expecting something like that. There could be no other reason why Monali would refuse to get married, except if she was already in love with someone, and knew that her parents would not approve of her choice.

"How?" I asked. I wasn't sure how I could help in this endeavour.

"We have set up a date next week with the registrar of marriages in Bandra. On that day, we will go to the registrar's office, sign the papers, and be married. We will need a witness. Jagan is getting Ketu, his sister. I will take you," Monali said. That thought made her smile more.

"And of course her Baba shouldn't know about it at all," Jagan said.

On the appointed day, the three of us took an autorickshaw to Bandra, and both signed a document in the presence of the registrar. I signed as a witness. Monali and Jagan then exchanged garlands. We went to a studio to take photographs.

Rajubhai was furious. He threw his chappal at me. I ducked in time and it hit the framed image of Ganapati, which Rajubhai garlanded every day; that at once subdued him. But he couldn't stop cursing. I had never heard him curse in this manner before. These were choice abuses, both original and devastatingly crude, describing in gory detail what would happen to my genitalia, except that he was getting the gender wrong. I listened to him in utter mystification. I was scared but I was also fascinated. This experience had immense educational value—I was learning a full range of extremely imaginative abuses but was certain that I wouldn't ever be able to use them.

After they were married, Monali moved into Jagan's home, which was in our neighbourhood. Jagan's family comprised of his parents and his younger sister. The senior Bendres—Jagan's parents—were not in favour of the marriage either, because they had already chosen "a nice CKP girl" for Jagan, and this "love marriage" business with a Mali-caste girl would definitely bring ignominy. But they couldn't protest much, because Jagan was the sole earner in the family. When their daughter told them about Jagan's marriage to Monali, they decided to return to Dharwad, where they had come from three decades ago.

Jagan, Monali, and his sister Ketu had the house to themselves. It was originally a bungalow owned by someone called Martin D'Souza.

I helped Monali move to Jagan's home and to rearrange the old and creaky furniture of the house to her preference. Jagan's friends from the neighbourhood, Abdul and Babu, came over to help. As we were unpacking and rearranging boxes, and putting them on the wooden shelves, a few men walked in. Abdul knew what they had come for.

"What do you want?" he asked.

In response, a man picked up a metal chair and threw it at Jagan. He ducked in time. Babu lifted a chair, swung it around, and ran to the street to get help. Abdul pushed Monali into another room and shut the door. He also flung a chair at the intruders. They ran away, but on their way out they knifed Jagan in the back and hit him on the head with a cricket bat. Jagan fainted. Babu and Abdul rushed him to Cooper Hospital in Abdul's taxi.

I stood there transfixed with fear. I didn't know what to do. From the other room, Monali screamed at me to open the door. She rushed out with me and we followed Babu and Abdul to the hospital in an autorickshaw. I was certain that Rajubhai had orchestrated the attack, and I said so to Monali. She was weeping uncontrollably.

"I didn't think he would do something like that," she said.

The doctor at the emergency ward said Jagan's wound was deep, and he wasn't sure if he would survive. When she heard that,

Monali's sorrow transformed into anger and hatred for her father.

"I will kill him. Yes, I will kill him, for sure," Monali said. Her voice was faint as a whisper, but her eyes were blazing.

Dadi and Sadanand Kaka had heard about the morning's incident but were not sure what to do. Dadi didn't know Jagan or Monali, and Sadanand Kaka was conflicted—Rajubhai was a friend, and he couldn't believe that his friend would turn against his daughter and hire goons to murder his son-in-law.

"You don't have to be involved in all this," Dadi said.

"No, Dadi. I am involved and I will help Monali," I said, as firmly as I could, and for once my grandmother kept quiet. Nobody had trusted me as Monali had, and nobody had treated me with greater affection. I would stand by her and wouldn't let my Dadi talk me out of that. I was an adult now, and earning too, although I was certain Rajubhai would sack me.

When I reached the hospital, Monali was sitting by herself on a bench outside the intensive care ward. Jagan was barely conscious, he had a broken rib, a fractured right arm, and a deep and wide knife wound in the lower back; his head had been split open by the blow from the cricket bat.

"The bleeding has stopped, but the wounds will take a long time to heal," Monali said, looking anxious.

Abdul and Babu reached the hospital soon after, and they coaxed Monali to go home and take a break.

"Go home, eat something, rest for a while, and return in the afternoon," Babu said.

"I will talk to your father," Abdul said.

Monali looked at them uncertainly and reluctantly agreed.

Then, looking at Babu and me, Abdul said, "Let's go to talk to Rajubhai."

"No, leave Sharad out of it, he is just a kid," Babu said.

"I am not a kid," I protested.

"Okay. But you go with Monali and make sure she is safe." When he put it that way, it was impossible to say no. I accompanied Monali to her home.

"Do you know whose men they were?" she asked.

"Most probably the Shiv Sena mob," I said. "They had to be from somewhere nearby."

When we reached Jagan's home, Rajubhai and a few men were waiting for us. Monali clutched at my hand when she saw them. At the door, Rajubhai walked up to her and tried to hug her. She pushed him away as hard as she could and he fell. He struggled to get back up, then he lunged at her, grabbing her throat, and choking her. I tried to pull him away from her, but the men who had come with him pushed me aside and the tallest of them slapped me hard across my face. I went deaf momentarily and felt the world spin around me before I collapsed in a heap.

"Don't you dare do anything to him," Monali screamed.

"Pandu, hit him till he dies," Rajubhai shouted hysterically. "And all of you, drag her into the car."

The men immediately lifted Monali and ran to the car.

Pandu, fair-skinned and tall as a film star, wearing a safari jacket and bell-bottom trousers, walked up to me, offered me a hand, and lifted me to my feet.

"*Beta*, don't get into trouble with these rich people."

I stared at him; the sun was in my eyes and I couldn't see him properly.

"Keep your eyes down," Pandu whispered and tapped me on the forehead.

One of Pandu's men hit me on the back of my head. I don't

know what I was thinking, but I was so enraged that I punched him in his gut.

"*Saale*, you dare hit my man. *Saale chutiye*, you are finished!" Pandu shouted.

Pandu's men pounced on me and wrestled me flat to the ground—some holding my neck, others my arms, my legs, and someone else dug a heel into my crotch. I shrieked in pain, but I just got angrier instead of getting scared.

Pandu bent down and yelled into my ears: "*Bhenchod*, we can kill you right now, and nobody would know."

I spit on his face.

In a blind rage, Pandu slashed my forehead with a sharp stone and punched me so hard that I passed out. I don't know for how long I lay in the compound of Martin D'Souza's bungalow, but it couldn't have been too long. The afternoon sun revived me. I managed to walk to Dr Mankodi's clinic. He immediately called for a taxi and sent his compounder with me to Dr Gala's Nursing Home near Andheri station. I must have passed out again on the way, because when I opened my eyes, Abdul, Bala, Dadi, Sadanand Kaka, and Neeta were standing beside the bed.

The smell of chloroform and disinfectant made me nauseous and dizzy. The room was painted white and everything else inside the room was white too—the curtains, the bed, a small table beside the bed. My face was swollen and bruised. My right arm was in a cast and my head and upper body were heavily bandaged. I felt tired.

"You will be all right," Abdul said reassuringly. "Your wounds are superficial, except the one on the forehead, where they have had to stitch you up."

"He cut me with a stone," I mumbled, and found it was difficult for me to speak.

"Where is Monali?" Babu asked, sounding urgent.

"Rajubhai and his men took her away in his car," I said. "Then

Pandu and his men beat me."

"You take rest," Abdul said. "We have to go and get Monali."

After they left, Dadi sat beside me.

"How long do I have to be here?"

"I don't know, at least till all that swelling on your face is reduced."

The sedatives given to me ensured that I didn't stay awake for long. In the evening I was gently woken up by my grandmother.

"I told you not to get involved," she said, looking at me pitifully. "See what they have done to you."

"Dadi, I did what was right."

"Really, and do you think your new friends would help you if you needed help?" she asked, and after a moment, answered her own question. "Actually, they have. Abdul is paying the hospital bills."

I got discharged in a couple of days and then stayed at home for a week, during which time Monali came to visit me every day.

I went to their home after Jagan returned from the hospital. And that is when Abdul and Babu narrated to me all that had happened.

Abdul and Babu went to the hospital to see Jagan, but he was still going in and out of consciousness. They decided to go to Rajubhai's office, but he wasn't there, so they went to his home, which was a new bungalow in the newly developed Sahar Road. The international airport had brought with it housing complexes, and a series of bungalows. Rajubhai, with his newfound wealth, had been among the first settlers. His bungalow had tall and ornate iron gates with a security guard. Abdul told him that he was a car mechanic from a nearby garage and he had come with his manager to estimate the cost of repairing one of the vintage cars that would be used for shooting. The guard let them in. There was no one on the ground floor of the bungalow. They stealthily climbed a huge curving staircase.

Suddenly, they heard footsteps and Abdul pushed Babu into the shadows.

Babu whispered, "That is Rajubhai."

Abdul ran to him and pushed him down. He gripped Rajubhai's mouth with his hand and punched him in the ribs a couple of times to knock the wind out of him. Babu crouched beside him and said, "We are Dhinmant Desai's friends, I am Babu and he is Abdul. Jagan is in hospital. You paid some goons to beat him up. He nearly died."

Terrified and motionless, Rajubhai stared at them. Babu pulled him up.

"Don't do it again," Abdul said. "Or we will do it to you."

Monali, when she heard the commotion, came out of her room. And when she saw Abdul and Babu, she came running to them. Together, they quickly left the mansion, waving to the guard at the gate on their way out. The guard tried to raise an alarm when he saw Monali, but Babu's quick thinking saved them.

"She is coming with us for a part; we will be back soon."

When they returned to the hospital, Jagan was awake.

"So, where are you all coming from?" he asked.

"We went to Rajubhai's house."

"And what did you do?" Jagan said, his voice rising.

"We had to get Monali back," Babu said.

Jagan groaned. "How are we going to handle all this?"

But it was handled quite easily and smoothly. Abdul spoke to Dhinmant, and the two went to meet Rajubhai at the studio. In less than ten minutes the man agreed to accept his daughter's marriage to Jagan.

"How did he agree so easily?" Monali asked Abdul.

"He didn't have a choice. We unionized his staff and called for a strike. He agreed to everything."

Rain

The journey from Delhi to Bareilly on the Kashi Vishwanath Express was not comfortable, even in my first-class compartment. It was hot and got hotter. I was on my way to Bahedi to work as a storekeeper at the local sugar factory. I was already having doubts about the job, though I didn't have a choice. My family's finances were getting tighter.

Working for Rajubhai was okay for a while, but the money wasn't good enough. Moreover, Monali no longer worked for her father, and Rajubhai's attitude towards me had changed after the high drama involving his daughter and son-in-law. I was left with no choice but to quit. Abdul and Bala promised to help me but couldn't come up with anything concrete.

Although Baba had left us many years ago, the government continued to pay some pension, which helped Dadi manage our home expenses. She supplemented that income by preparing lunchboxes and using the *dabbawallah* network to feed some two dozen officegoers. But Ma's condition had deteriorated rapidly and Dadi had decided to move her to a sanatorium in Khandala. This was probably necessary, because Dadi didn't have the time—or the patience—to look after Ma, who needed constant attention.

By now Ma had acute rheumatoid arthritis, which confined her to bed. Lately, she also showed signs of dementia. Dadi had spoken to Sadanand Kaka, who knew a trustee at the sanatorium. "It wouldn't cost us much," Dadi muttered when I said that it would probably be better if we just kept Ma with us. "Keeping her here will be more expensive," she said, in a tone that discouraged any discussion on the subject. But the sanatorium cost, even after all the discounts, was becoming unaffordable on just my father's pension and Dadi's lunch services; and though Dadi didn't say anything, it was clear from her sullenness that she wanted me to take up a job.

I couldn't get anything in Bombay. A storekeeper's position in the sugar factory at Bahedi was available, and reluctantly I accepted it. The group that interviewed me—the factory's general manager and other officials from the head office—assured me that the job wouldn't be difficult. I would of course have to move to Bahedi to the factory's housing colony. I didn't have good feelings about the job even when I accepted it. I didn't see any positives in the situation except that I would be paid a salary, and my Dadi would find her life slightly easier.

So here I was, at the end of the summer, in India's most populated state, far away from my hometown. The air was heavy with damp. I felt like getting right back onto the train coach and returning to Bombay. As I was struggling with my bags, I saw a man with a placard bearing my name. I waved at him and he rushed to take them from me. He led me to a car, a white Ambassador with a small fan on the dashboard whirring furiously. I sat in the front beside Narayan, the driver.

Narayan had a big smile with a row of neat white teeth looking more pronounced on his dark-skinned face. He wore a loose white uniform. His nose was a thin straight line on his face, which seemed like a perfect circle. He was taller than me and thinner. He instructed me not to open the car window. "That will let the dust inside," he said. He tried to make the drive interesting by his constant chatter. He had been working with the factory for as long as he could remember and was eager to tell me all that he thought I needed to know. Before long, I was unable to keep my eyes open and dozed off.

A strange smell awoke me and I checked my wristwatch; we had been on the road for an hour.

"It's the smell of molasses; we have reached the sugar factory," Narayan said, anticipating my question.

I glanced outside the car window; it had begun to drizzle. The terrain had transformed from arid flatland and consisted now of a thick foliage of trees and shrubs, but it wasn't natural wild growth. The trees and shrubs were like ornaments, nurtured for their looks. The factory comprised of massive structures to the left of the two-lane highway; to the right were the housing quarters for the workers. A line of trucks overloaded with sugarcane was waiting to enter the factory.

Narayan turned the car into a street with rows of houses on both sides and lined with more trees. But for the horrible stench, this was a place straight out of a children's picture book. He drove me to the farthest corner of the housing quarters and stopped outside an ancient-looking bungalow. This guesthouse was to be my temporary home. It was decrepit. The strong smell of molasses was now mixed with the smell of wet earth. The drizzle had turned into a steady downpour.

"I will go and get an umbrella, you wait in the car," Narayan said, but I got off and I ran inside.

"You will be living here in the guesthouse till a house is vacated,"

Narayan said, as he hurriedly ran after me, carrying my bags.

The guesthouse was spacious; it had wooden floors and a broad verandah in the front. A wide corridor opened into many rooms; one of them was the dining room.

"That door leads to the field behind the house, it is shut, always," Narayan said, pointing towards the far end.

He led me to a big room with a high ceiling, from which, rather precariously, hung a fan that began to rotate and screech when Narayan turned it on. He switched on the lights. The room was now well-lit. It had large French windows on one side, covering the entire wall, which bathed the room in daylight and gave a panoramic view of the field outside. There was a large bed, covered by a mosquito net, a desk with a lamp and chair, and a couch. A door led to a bathroom.

Narayan spoke in a singsong manner and in short bursts, the pitch of his voice varying, as he moved both his hands.

"This is your room; I will serve you your meal in about an hour, nothing special—simple dal, roti. We serve meat only during the weekends. Then, tomorrow morning, breakfast—it will be eggs, toast, and tea. After that, I will take you to the factory office to meet Khan Saab. Now I am going to the kitchen to cook—ring the bell if you need anything and don't open the windows or you will let the mosquitos in," he said.

I walked over to the French windows. There was a large backyard with manicured grass. Beyond that was a vast open field. I went into the bathroom to change into a kurta-pyjama. The bathroom was extraordinarily large—almost as large as my Teli Gali home in Bombay. It had three half-open ventilators and a small washbasin that had yellowed with age.

The stench of molasses crept into the bathroom, which was

surprising because my room smelled only of disinfectants. The sound of raindrops on the roof was constant but muted and couldn't drown the drone of crickets outside. A house lizard crawled on the bathroom wall.

The furnishing of the bungalow, its furniture, the fan, the ceiling light, and the table lamp all belonged to another era, when space was not a premium. The guesthouse was grand and distinctly ancient in an aristocratic way.

I returned to the living room and sat on the couch, which had a musty smell, and began reading the James Hadley Chase thriller I had bought at the Bombay Central station. After a while, the silence became oppressive, overbearing. I found it hard to focus on the novel. I dozed off and awoke to find Narayan standing beside me, calling my name.

"What time is it?" I asked.

"Time for dinner."

He led me to the dining room. The furniture, as in other rooms, belonged to an era long gone. Two ornate chandeliers hung from the ceiling. I sat on one of the high-backed plush dining chairs covered in dark green leather. The dining table was dark mahogany. An old grandfather clock, with a humungous pendulum moving languorously, ticked tiredly near the door. On the walls hung four rotating fans—two on each side, and between them hung landscape paintings depicting English countrysides.

Dinner was simple but sumptuous, as Narayan had promised. For dessert, he had made a custard pudding, which was delicious but seemed out of place with the distinctly Indian menu.

"The cutlery used to be silver and the plates were bone china, but Khan Saab switched to stainless steel a few years ago," Narayan said, without hiding his disapproval.

It hadn't stopped raining. Now the sound of raindrops on the roof was louder and mingled with the occasional croak from a frog. I returned to my room and lay down on the bed. I tried to read but found it hard to focus. I fell asleep.

A sharp clap of thunder woke me, lightning ceaselessly snaking through the sky lighting up the room every few seconds. The rain was torrential, it sounded like a million pellets hitting the roof. I heard a strange, unfamiliar sound above the monsoon din. It came from the corridor. Someone or something was scraping the wooden floor, dragging something heavy. I switched on the table lamp and sat up on the bed, but the sound faded. It must be Narayan, I thought, moving something. But I wondered why he should do so at this time. I drifted to sleep surrounded by the magical music of the monsoon.

I woke up when Narayan came in with tea.

I glanced out of the window. It was still dark. The rain hadn't stopped.

"Did you sleep well?" he asked.

"What were you pulling through the corridor?"

"Nothing," he said, and then he froze. His eyes widened and he seemed unnerved.

"But Saab, that can't be . . . he comes only during the late monsoon, never this early. It must be because it has been raining nonstop since yesterday," he said, looking at the door and then leaning back to look into the corridor.

"Who?"

"Arthur hates to get wet. Those were his footsteps you heard," Narayan said, then shuddered and glanced again at the door and the corridor.

"Who is Arthur?"

"The ghost," Narayan said, as if referring to an old acquaintance.

"What do you mean, the ghost? Is this house haunted?" I asked.

The cup of tea nearly fell out of my hands, spilling as I abruptly sat up on the bed.

"Don't worry. Arthur is harmless," Narayan said, but he didn't seem convinced himself.

"You mean there is a real ghost here?" I said in nervous excitement.

"Arthur doesn't live here," Narayan said, and when he saw my face, he quickly added, "I mean, he only comes in when it rains heavily."

"Stop talking like that," I said, my voice at a high pitch. I gulped the tea quickly. I was scared rather than excited.

The storehouse was located next to the factory. It appeared large from the outside and had recently been painted yellow. Its roof sloped on two sides and was covered with light brown tiles. The walls were brick. The place was breezy and dry because of the dozen industrial fans whirring furiously inside. There were rows of mechanical parts placed on iron racks.

The storekeeper, Mustafa Khan, was a small man in a white shirt and black trousers. The shirt was starched crisp, the trousers were meticulously ironed. He welcomed me with a nod and shook my hand. I looked around as he led me to my work desk.

My job was to help him maintain inventory. I didn't have to move anything physically; for that there were many helpers. There were a number of machinists in the store, and some of the helpers assisted them in getting the parts they wanted. The others, who had all lined up with Mustafa near the door to greet me, had now reclaimed their chairs.

"Narayan told me that you have already met our friend Arthur," Mustafa said, raising his eyebrows and smiling.

"Yes, I believe so," I said, and looked at him, wondering if he was joking or serious.

"We have had many new recruits leave because of him," Mustafa said.

I nodded again. Both Mustafa and Narayan spoke of the ghost as if they knew him intimately.

"It is a bit disconcerting, you will agree," I said.

"Oh, you shouldn't worry at all," Mustafa said, waving a hand to reassure me, but I wasn't convinced. It is one thing to read ghost stories or see horror movies, and quite another to meet a ghost.

"So, what is the story, is this ghost for real?" I asked.

"Yes, if you believe and no, if you don't. Local lore has it that the ghost is of a British soldier killed in a battle during the 1857 uprising," Mustafa said, and then he began to explain the inventory logs for machine parts that the store maintained, and how I was to update them. The ghost was no longer a subject of interest.

Mustafa obviously didn't expect too much from me. I feared the job would be excruciatingly boring. He busied himself with his own tasks with an air of importance. He spoke to me only during the lunch hour, when we walked from the store to the guesthouse to have our meal which Narayan had cooked. I noticed that there were no trees this side of the factory, but shrubs lined both sides of the street.

Mustafa spoke about his interest in ghazals and the great poets and singers. I knew nothing about ghazals and couldn't care less, but politely kept quiet and nodded occasionally to not seem disinterested. He spoke about movies and lamented that there was only one cinema house in Bahedi, which screened old films.

"I go to Bareilly to see the latest movies at least once a month," he said.

I nodded. All I could think of was the overpowering stench of molasses in open pits; it was revolting and pervasive. I wondered how people could let it become an integral part of their lives.

After work, Mustafa took me to the factory's *gymkhana*, an indoor sports and workout place that also doubled as a community centre. Mustafa told me that every evening after work most of the families of senior staff gathered here for dinner.

Above the main door of the *gymkhana* were mounted animal heads from hunting expeditions. They looked ancient. A large wooden panel listed the names of the factory managers from 1912 onward; the Brits had managed the factory for a long time, even after India's independence.

"How long will it take for a house to be allotted to me?" I asked.

"Generally, within three months, after your confirmation, but bachelors get a room, only families get houses. I think you are better off at the guesthouse," Mustafa said.

That evening, Mustafa asked me whether he could accompany me to the guesthouse because, he said, it was my first day, and we could both do with some conversation. Mustafa asked Narayan to serve drinks. He walked out to the verandah, but Narayan told him to sit inside the room.

"The mosquitos will have a feast," Narayan said.

Mustafa sipped his rum and Coca-Cola quietly, perhaps too quietly for my liking. I asked him about his family. He didn't seem keen to talk about them.

"So, what is the story about this ghost?" I asked.

"A lot of it is folklore and superstition," he said. "When I came here, about twenty-seven years ago, and when I heard of this ghost, I went to Lucknow to look up the local archives. There is nothing specific about the ghost, but historical records suggest that the factory's complex stands on what was a battlefield during the 1857 rebellion. The Indian rebels led by Khan Bahadur Khan fought the British army's Highland Brigade led by Captain Campbell. That is about all that I could learn," Mustafa said.

He called Narayan to join us. "Make a drink for yourself, too, and tell Sharad about your friend," Mustafa said.

Narayan was delighted at the suggestion and wasted no time in pouring a stiff drink for himself—the same as mine, Indian whisky and club soda with ice.

"It is a long story, sir," he said as he sat down.

"We have all evening before us," Mustafa said.

Narayan smiled and began his narration.

"I heard it when I came here from Belgaum," he said, his voice quavering. "I was surprised that the management wanted me to sign a three-year bond. You see, the other housekeepers had left hurriedly; one of them even left his bags behind. I remember the first time I saw him was when Doctor Chouhan was here."

"Yuvraj Chouhan turned the factory's dispensary and the first-aid centre into a hospital," Mustafa said. "He was a fine doctor, a bachelor."

"Narayan, I want to know about the ghost," I gently nudged him.

"Oh yes, yes. It was raining. I was doing the dishes. I heard footsteps in the corridor and came out of the kitchen to check. I froze at what I saw. There was this tall *gora* officer, wearing a red coat, white trousers. His trousers were covered in mud, and blood dripped from his coat. I stood rooted to the ground," Narayan said, and shivered.

"You actually saw him. It wasn't a mirage?" I asked.

"No, no, real. He walked up to me, from the far side of the corridor, and even spoke to me," Narayan said, gulping down his drink hurriedly. Clearly, the memory of that encounter still rattled him.

"What did he say?" I asked.

"'My wound hurts more in the rain,' he said, and as he was turning back, Dr Chouhan came out of his room.

"'What is all this commotion?' he asked me.

"The soldier walked up to him and said, 'I am Arthur Birkenshaw from the Highland Brigade.'"

"Both of you must have peed in your pants," Mustafa said with a chuckle. He wasn't taking any of this seriously, perhaps because he had heard it many times.

Narayan was now deeply involved in his story and poured himself another stiff drink. He sat down to continue his tale.

"Now, this Dr Chouhan had presence of mind. He offered his hand to the soldier, but the soldier was clutching at his stomach.

"'You are bleeding,' the doctor said, looking at the soldier's wound.

"'My wound hurts more in the rain,' the soldier said.

"'I am a doctor. Do you need help?' Doctor Saab asked him.

"'My wound hurts more in the rain,' the soldier repeated.

"Doctor Saab turned to me and said, 'Narayan, let us leave the man alone. Come inside.' I was shivering intensely and was so rooted to the spot that the doctor had to drag me in," Narayan said, his voice rising to a high pitch. He looked at us again, studying our faces for our reactions.

"That is it?" I asked, unable to hide my disappointment. This was rather dull and anticlimactic.

"What did you expect? Some more flashes of lightning and thunder?" Mustafa asked, and chuckled.

"If you had seen him you would react differently," Narayan said, a bit defensively. "After that night, I often heard the steps in the corridor but didn't see him. He frightens me always, but I gradually taught myself to ignore him, take no notice. I don't get in his way, and he has never crossed mine. He comes inside only when it rains heavily."

The door to my room was wide open. I couldn't be sure what time it was but it was well past midnight. I remembered closing the door to my room after Mustafa had left in a drunken stupor; it was ajar now. I got up to shut it again. As soon as I did so, I heard footsteps in the corridor. The sound was distinct, sharp, and uncomfortably close; someone was walking in the corridor and had stopped right outside the room. A moment later, the door swung open.

My heart was pounding and I was sweating and shivering. I clutched at the door for support and stood transfixed, too frightened to move. I didn't see anyone but I heard footsteps; someone or something had entered my room and had walked from the door to the French windows. I still couldn't see anything, and after standing at the door for what felt like a long time, I forced myself to slowly walk to the bed. I was determined to talk to Narayan, and to Mustafa, too. I couldn't possibly keep living in this place.

I lay awake for a long time and then drifted back to a whisky-induced sleep. I woke up some time later that night when I heard the rumble of thunder outside; streaks of lightning lit up the room sporadically. I got up and walked to the water pitcher that Narayan had placed on the table, poured myself a glass of water. That is when I saw a silhouette of someone standing beside the door. The glass of water fell from my hand and crashed to the floor, breaking into pieces. The person walked away; his breathing was heavy and distinctly audible over the monsoon din.

"I couldn't be out in the rain. I have this wound that hurts more in rains," the man was saying, his voice soft, his accent English.

I heard myself scream before I fainted. Moments later, when I opened my eyes, Narayan was beside me. He helped me to the bed. It was still dark and it was still raining.

"It is okay. He was here. I heard him, too. He is gone now. Your scream must have scared him," Narayan said, and smiled at me sympathetically.

"I can't live here. I am going, leaving tomorrow," I said.

"But why?" he asked, clearly incredulous.

"What do you mean why? I just saw a ghost."

"But *you* scared him away."

Activist

I asked Sanjana why she used her father's car when it was clear that he would not be supportive of her concerns. "Sharad, my purpose in life is to redistribute my father's wealth among poor people," she said. I didn't detect any irony in her voice. She looked at me to gauge my reaction. I didn't react; had I done so she would have continued with her irritating bombast.

I was the only journalist she had called to cover her protest march against the city's municipal administration for not supplying a water connection to the Bhima Nagar slum colony next to the Andheri flyover. Sanjana had formed the Bhima Nagar Slum People's Association in 1982 to prevent the demolition of the slums. Her struggle had ensured that the slum wasn't demolished, and now she was demanding a piped water connection there.

Sanjana Pardi was charismatic with an earthy appeal. In her mid-thirties, she was thin, short, sprightly. Her hair was wiry and disheveled, and her hooded eyes were sparkly, hinting mischief. Her nose was straight and pointed like an arrow and her chin jutted out. She wore khadi kurtas and jeans and carried a *jhola*. Sanjana dressed as an archetypal, almost clichéd, activist, and the only thing missing about her was Kolhapuri chappals. She preferred Bata sandals.

She grabbed my arm and led me through the gathering of the slum people.

"Look at these people, Sharad, they are human beings. You journalists call them slum dwellers. It is a description that makes them faceless and reduces them to a mere statistic," she said, raising her voice to be heard above the din of the restless crowd.

She climbed up onto a makeshift platform and began addressing the crowd. She had a mesmerizing effect. It was not what she said, but the way she said it that had her audience enthralled. She became one with the people by speaking their language—Bombay's street lingo: slangy and colloquial, and peppered with *gaalis* and jokes.

After the brief speech, she walked among the people, joining her hands in namaste, identifying most of them by their names, hugging women, kissing a child, warmly greeting men, but from a distance.

"You are building yourself to be a politician," I said.

"You are too cynical. These are my people."

I laughed. That annoyed her.

"Sharad, you should know the difference between politicians and activists. In the past they were the same, Gandhi and Ambedkar were both politicians and activists. But in our times, politicians are people who rise from the grassroots and reach exalted positions. They first make a lot of money and then occasionally think of solving people's problems."

"So how are activists different?" I asked.

"Generally, activists are people who have no aspirations to become politicians; they are educated, from the middle class, and genuinely interested in people," she said.

"You are wealthy," I said.

"I would call it an accident of birth, but it isn't," she said somewhat enigmatically.

"What do you mean?"

"Oh, that's a long story. Let's save it for another day." She asked her driver to take me to the tabloid office in Colaba where I worked.

Sanjana intrigued me. I knew her professionally. It would have seemed that we were friends, but I was a journalist in need of stories, and she was an up-and-coming activist in need of media exposure. Along with Dhinmant Desai, the fiery trade union leader, Sanjana was a rising star in Bombay's left world, an articulate champion of civil liberties, of the dispossessed, of fighting for the right causes.

I was merely a newcomer reporter who had recently joined the *Evening Standard*. She preferred to talk to me and not the other journalists because I believed in her. I was always in awe of her.

She was hotelier Dev Pardi's daughter and would potentially inherit a growing hospitality empire. She was living with Franklin Robinson, a civil liberties lawyer. Franklin, Sanjana said, was her "partner in life and work."

The chief reporter at the *Evening Standard*, Ganesh Vasudev Soni, readily agreed when I suggested that I do a profile on Sanjana. He was a classic old-school journalist, who had spent many years in obscurity at the *Times of India* as a reporter, in an era when reporters worked anonymously and were rarely, if ever, credited with a byline in print. But through years of nose-to-the-ground hard work, every journalist of that generation had acquired a formidable reputation.

GVS, as he was universally known, wore a white shirt (which he called a "bush coat") and black trousers to work every day. He greeted everyone with a brief smile, which seemed forced because of his lugubrious countenance and revealed his stained brown teeth that progressively acquired a darker hue each day because of excessive smoking and innumerable cups of tea. His eyes seemed to pop out of his thick, black-framed glasses that looked too small for his face.

He was delighted to have a profile of a young and upcoming female firebrand. I checked our tabloid archives about Dev Pardi, but the clippings mostly gave corporate information, nothing substantial about his personal life. The only sliver of personal history available was about his humble origins. He had shifted his base to Dubai and lived in Alankar Apartments in Andheri. I decided to follow that lead. I called Sanjana's office to check her whereabouts and found out that she was in Delhi for a meeting with the labour board. That was good. She wouldn't be around to realize—at least not immediately—that I was digging up her past.

Alankar Apartments in Andheri East was an old building across the Western Express Highway, next to Mohan Studio. It was being torn down to make way for a housing complex. At the gate I saw an elderly man with a cloth bag in his hand stuffed with vegetables. He was wearing a transparent white linen shirt (a *pehran*) and a white pyjama—the standard clothes a Gujarati man wore at home. He wore a religious thread across his shoulder. He eyed me suspiciously.

"Who do you want to meet?" he asked in English.

"Dev Pardi," I said.

The man looked at me sternly. "He hasn't lived here in decades," he said, in an accent that revealed both his education and prosperity. He looked at me uncertainly. After a moment's hesitation, he said, "Come with me. I am Rajendra Vasavada."

"Hello Mr Vasavada. I am Sharad," I said.

"Sharad what?"

"Sharad Sadashiv,"

"What is your surname?"

"Sir. I don't believe in using my surname, because it reveals my caste and unfairly categorizes me."

"You must be from the lower caste, then," he said, looking at me in a manner I found judgmental.

"What if I am? Will that make a difference in your attitude to me?"

"No. I am a proud follower of the Mahatma," he said, offering his hand. We shook hands and smiled. He led me inside the building, and we climbed up a flight of stairs. I followed him down a corridor and to his place.

"Let me apologize to you," he said as we sat down. "People from my generation always give their full names—first and last names. But then, in those days, things were different."

"The situation is no different now, sir. It is just that I have never been comfortable with caste identities."

"Yes, but let us not get sidetracked into that debate," Mr Vasavada said. "Tell me, why do you want to meet Dev Pardi? You seem sensibly well-informed to know that he wouldn't be living here. He is one of the richest men in India. Why should he live amidst such squalor?"

Old-world decency compelled Rajendra Vasavada to admit a mistake and display a charming affability to be unfazed by it and carry on a conversation.

"Mr Vasavada, I am a journalist, and I am working on a news story about Dev Pardi's life before he became who he became," I said.

"Everyone calls me Rajendrabhai."

"He is a noble soul," Rajendrabhai said, and became pensive. He looked at me intently, and then said, "He saved the life of an infant by adopting her when her parents died . . . committed suicide."

"You mean Sanjana Pardi?"

"Yes. It is not known to the public, and I don't think you should reveal it," Rajendrabhai said, sounding anxious. I noticed that he was completely bald. His narrow eyes were sharp and hadn't aged. He had a thin moustache that had turned white, and he had Mickey Mouse ears. His hands moved energetically as he spoke, and his voice was a deep baritone.

"I know Sanjana, and I came in search of her roots," I said.

Rajendrabhai was all perked up when he heard this and looked at me inquiringly.

"She hinted that Dev Pardi is not her father."

Rajendrabhai did not speak but his expression changed from polite condescension to guarded alertness. His eyes, which periodically danced and darted around the room, now steadied and he gazed at me intently. After a pause that didn't seem to end, during which I cleared my throat many times, the last one loudly, Rajendrabhai also cleared his throat.

"How long did Dev Pardi live here . . . in this building?" I asked.

"He was born here, and he left this building when he got a job in Umbergoan to manage a resort . . . that was about three decades ago," Rajendrabhai said.

"How long was he here?"

"Two decades, yes," he said.

"Did you know him well?"

"Yes, we are friends. We went to the same school and played cricket in the railway yard behind our building."

"How did he become so successful?" I asked.

"People say hard work makes fortunes, hard work and luck. In

Dev's case it was being in the right place at the right time," he said. Then, having realized that he was being far too candid for his own good, he suddenly turned to me and exclaimed, "If you want to know more about this matter, go and talk to Datta Mahale."

"The politician? How is he connected to this?" I asked.

"Talk to him and you will find out. And don't tell either him or Sanjana that I told you to do so." He got up from his chair and signaled an end to the conversation.

I returned to the office and delved into Datta Mahale's clippings file. He was a legislator in the state assembly from Dombivili, then a distant suburb, now a part of Bombay, the bustling megapolis that begins on the edge of the Arabian Sea and doesn't end. He had been re-elected four times. I called his office telephone and requested that his assistant schedule an appointment with him at his party office in Bombay. The assistant was delighted that a journalist wanted to meet his boss and scheduled the meeting for the next afternoon. He gave me a lot of information about his boss, none of which was relevant to Sanjana or Dev Pardi. I was not interested in the achievements of Datta Mahale as a "leader with a mass following."

Datta Mahale had a thick black moustache and paan-stained lips. His white hair matched the linen kurta-pyjama he wore. He was in his late fifties or early sixties. His eyes were lined with kohl. A thick gold chain hung around his neck. He wiped his face with a small white towel but continued to sweat profusely. He smiled as he took me into his opulent office and went on to sit on a plush chair upholstered in white faux leather. His table, made of wood and glass, was spotlessly clean—it had no papers on it and the only prominent object was a green telephone. His assistant brought two cups of tea and a plate of biscuits. Datta began to sip his tea, making loud slurping sounds.

"My assistant told me that you wanted to talk to me for your newspaper," he said.

"I want to know more about the relationship between Sanjana and Dev Pardi," I said. His face instantly transformed into a menacing scowl, and he dropped his half-eaten biscuit into the waste bin below his table.

"I don't have time for all this," he said, and got up.

"Datta Saab, please. I am not doing a report on this subject. I just want to know what exactly their relationship is, because Sanjana hinted that she is not Dev Pardi's daughter," I said, speaking rapidly.

I don't know what made him stop in his tracks and look at me disdainfully.

"You journalists don't have any respect for other people's lives. Sanjana is not a film star whom you should be snooping around to dig up dirt about her personal life," he said.

"I am merely checking the veracity of what she hinted."

"And who told you to talk to me?"

"Rajendra Vasavada from Alankar Apartments, but he told me not to tell you that he was the one who made the suggestion," I said, trying to sound both earnest and abject.

Datta walked back and sat on the chair. His demeanour changed back to amiable.

"That old man will always be a troublemaker," he said. He looked at me intently, then after a pause, he said, "Sanjana is my niece. But before you put this or anything else in the newspaper, please check with her. She doesn't want anyone to know that I am her uncle. She finds me embarrassing," he said, and looked at me intently to gauge my reaction.

Stupefied, I gaped at him.

Speaking slowly, Datta said, "Dev Pardi is not Sanjana's father.

If you want to know more, get Sanjana with you and come and meet me with her. Or talk to Dev Pardi."

I had reached a dead end. The only way forward was to talk to Sanjana, because it was impossible to establish contact with Dev Pardi. He had no reason to talk to me. I was certain she would be furious to find out that I was snooping around about her personal life. Still, I called Sanjana that evening.

"Sure, come over now if you want, I have just returned from Delhi, and I have a remarkable story for you," she said.

"Sanjana, I don't want a story right now, I want to talk to you about yourself," I said. I heard her breathe heavily and she asked, "What about me?"

"I have met Rajendra Vasavada and Datta Mahale," I said.

There was a brief silence, then Sanjana shrieked, "You bastard; you fucking jerk, what the fuck do you think you are doing? My personal life is none of your goddamn business, you demented freak!" She hung up before I could say anything.

Her reaction frightened me. I sat numbly by the phone for some time, not sure what to do, and then went home feeling morose and guilty. I began writing a letter to Dev Pardi, explaining to him my desire to know the truth. I made a carbon copy. It was a short letter, and I introduced myself and briefly explained my quest to know the truth about his relationship with Sanjana. I said that I didn't plan to use the information in any news report. The next morning, I dropped the letter at Dev Pardi's corporate headquarters, and I mailed the carbon copy to Sanjana.

I began working on other assignments, trying to forget my pursuit of Sanjana's personal life. I met Franklin at the labour court a couple of days later, and he gave me a knowing sort of a smile. I didn't dare to ask him anything and waved at him half-heartedly.

He waved back, didn't seem eager to talk, and walked away into the lawyers' room.

A couple of days later, one of my colleagues informed me that Sanjana had called and left a message for me to call her back. I immediately did so.

"Come over this evening if you are free, I am having a get-together with friends," she said, sounding friendly.

When I reached her place in Santacruz, Sanjana and Franklin were waiting for me in the living room. They took me to the terrace where a group of people sat stiffly. I saw Rajendrabhai and Datta Mahale and an elderly couple; it took me some moments to figure out that the man was Dev Pardi. He looked smaller and paler than his photographs. I presumed that the woman was Dev Pardi's wife. I looked at them hesitantly.

"Come on in," Sanjana said, her voice betraying slight unease. Pointing at Dev Pardi and the woman with him, she said, "My dad and mom."

I greeted them with a namaste and sat down. Dev Pardi and his wife were sitting on a large couch; Rajendrabhai and Datta Mahale were sitting on a smaller couch. Sanjana handed me a glass of orange juice. From the fourth-floor terrace, I could see the slow-moving traffic below on SV Road.

"Let me not beat around the bush," she said. "After I received your letter, I thought long and hard about the nature of my relationship with my dad and mom. I spoke to Franklin and Rajendrabhai. Datta Mama also called me." She stopped and looked at Franklin and Dev for support.

"I told Sanjana to tell you everything," Dev Pardi said.

"He was probably scared of a scandal," Rajendrabhai said, and chuckled.

"I wasn't going to write about it," I said softly.

"Yes, Sanjana said so, but I don't trust the media," Dev Pardi said with effortless candour. "I don't want people to jump to any conclusions, especially the wrong ones," he added.

"Sanjana is Dev's and Urmi's adopted daughter," Rajendrabhai said, interrupting Dev Pardi, who was getting agitated.

"I gathered that much after I spoke to Datta Mahale and you," I said.

"You journalists should learn to mind your own business," Datta Mahale said, his voice rising slightly, unable to conceal his anger. Dev nodded vigorously in agreement. Datta wasn't quite finished yet and added, "And this is a personal matter, nothing to do with what either Dev, Sanjana, or I do in our public life."

"Okay, let us not turn this into a media ethics debate. We have all gathered here to present Sharad with the facts, so let us just do that," Franklin said calmly, and looked at Sanjana. She had recovered her poise and began.

"Sharad, my biological parents Ghanshyam and Manjula were star-crossed lovers. They were neighbours in Alankar Apartments, where my real parents Dev and Urmi also lived, as did Rajendrabhai and, of course, Datta Mama, who is my biological mother Manjula's brother." She said all this in one breath and then heaved a huge, almost interminable sigh.

"Please remember, I said my biological parents and my real parents. For some children, the real parents are not their biological ones," she said, looking intensely at me. Then she held Franklin's hand, again seeking his support.

Datta took over the narrative and came straight to the point, "Manjula and Ghanshyam fell in love, but their parents wouldn't agree to their plan to get married because Ghanshyam was a Brahmin from Uttar Pradesh and Manjula was a Kunbi from Maharashtra. So, with Rajendra's help, they eloped and got married.

They lived with Rajendra's aunt in Pune for a year or so. Manjula died because of some complications during Sanjana's birth."

"Ghanshyam was distraught, and the next day walked in front of a train," Rajendrabhai said.

"He blamed me for my mother's death," Sanjana said, in a low, soft voice.

"No, he didn't," Rajendrabhai said.

"In any case, Rajendrabhai asked Dev and Urmi to adopt me, and they were delighted to do so," Sanjana said.

"But we made the mistake of not telling her that she had been adopted," Urmi said, speaking for the first time.

"Because we wanted her to be our daughter, not an adopted one, but she discovered it accidentally a few years ago when she met Datta at a public event," Dev said.

"I was only trying to make her realize that she was my blood," Datta said, sounding apologetic.

"That was a fine way to do so," Sanjana said at a high pitch. "You blackmailed me into submission. I couldn't fight you publicly after you told me you were my uncle—my mother's brother," Sanjana said.

I was in the thick of a full-blown family drama, not following everything being said. Franklin sensed my confusion and helpfully intervened. He said, "Sanjana was fighting the Maharashtra government on the Adivasi people's right to their land and opposing a highway construction near Dahanu. Datta was supporting the highway, as it would connect the vegetable market to the farmers. And just when it seemed that the government would agree to Sanjana's demand and realign the highway, Datta came to meet us and told her about Manjula and Ghanshyam and requested Sanjana to withdraw the agitation and help her uncle."

"That hit me hard, and I withdrew from the agitation," Sanjana said softly.

"I was merely trying to explain to her the benefits of the highway," Datta said, again sounding apologetic, but his deceit wasn't lost on anyone.

"Ha!" Dev exclaimed, and Urmi put her hand on his to restrain him.

"I confronted my dad and mom, and they were forced to admit the truth. I dropped everything I was doing to learn the truth," Sanjana said. "I went to Alankar Apartments, only to learn from Rajendrabhai that Ghanshyam's parents had left the building almost at once after he ended his life, and they had probably returned to Allahabad. Datta Mama took me to meet his and my mother's mother—Aaji, who was overjoyed to see me, and wouldn't let me go from her embrace," Sanjana said. Tears streamed down her face and she held on tightly to Franklin.

I was with the family for a couple of hours and then Sanjana and Franklin dropped me home in her car. We didn't speak during the ride. I sent her flowers and a thank-you note a day later.

Elopement

Deepak's father Atmaram was killed in a freak accident. A truck turning from Teli Gali into Andheri-Kurla Road rammed into another coming the opposite way. Atmaram was crossing the road and was sandwiched between the two trucks. He had gone to the Teli Gali park to collect jasmine flowers for his visit to the Ganapati *mandir* nearby. He had followed this routine for many years. His gruesome death was a good reason, if one were needed, to be an atheist or at least remain an agnostic.

When I said this to Dadi, she frowned. "*Chup*, you fool," she said, curling her left palm into a fist and shaking her head.

Deepak and I shared our childhood and youth; we had grown up together in Teli Gali, playing cricket in the park, climbing trees, learning to swim in an abandoned well behind the park. To keep from drowning, we would each tie one end of a rope around our waists and the other to a tree. We would rent bicycles from Sardar Cycle Shop and cruise at breakneck speed on the dusty railway grain warehouse smelling of rotting wheat; we fell frequently, bruising our knees.

Deepak also helped me prepare for school exams; he was the studious one.

Childhood friends drift apart as they grow older, but their bond remain strong. When Deepak's father died in the accident, we were living different lives. I had been a journalist for a while, and he was working at the Grand Imperial Hotel. He had done a program in hotel management, something that wasn't considered normal then. Later he trained to become a chef. He began as a helper, but soon he was heading the hotel's main kitchen.

The Grand Imperial Hotel was a bit of an anomaly—it was a five-star hotel in a lower-middle-class neighbourhood. But it had a steady clientele from the film crowd. Teli Gali was in proximity to many film studios, and all the studios ordered food from the hotel.

All of Deepak's friends helped him with his father's funeral, and although we promised to meet more frequently, we returned to our separate worlds. We still cared for each other, but our lives had taken different directions.

A month after Atmaram's death, Deepak came to meet me one evening. I was at work, and he left word with Dadi. I went to meet him at his hotel on Thursday, my weekly day off. He served me a hot masala chai and a vegetable sandwich, after which we went to our old haunt, the Teli Gali park.

"Sharad, I need your help," Deepak said.

I nodded.

"Radhika and I want to get married."

"Radhika . . . Suresh Mama's daughter?"

He watched me for my reaction.

"How . . . ?"

"It's a long story. The short version is, we have been together for two years now."

"What do you mean 'together'?"

This was hard to accept. Radhika was the girl next door. She was younger than all of us, younger than Neeta, even. She was the young one we took care of, protected.

When you grow up together, you don't think of a girl as anything more than a friend, especially when she is the youngest. Yes, as you grow up into adolescence, you tend to become more gender-conscious, boys and girls forming separate groups. But girls you grow up with don't usually become objects of love or lust; they stay friends. And so when I learned about Deepak and Radhika, I was stunned.

"Look, Sharad, we need your help. We want to get married."

"Isn't she much younger than you . . . than us?"

"No . . . what do you mean? I am not marrying a child!" Deepak said with a pained look, sounding at once annoyed and defensive. He pulled out a photo from his wallet and thrust it into my face. Deepak and Radhika were smiling. I immediately saw that he was older—much older—than her.

"How can I help? The easiest way would be to go to the marriage registrar's office and register. You can get married in a month."

"She will be eighteen only later this year," he said.

"So, she is young," I said, and then quickly added, "Well, wait for her to be an adult."

"No, we can't wait. Her parents know about us and are planning to get her betrothed later this month," Deepak said anxiously.

I looked at him without hope. I didn't want to get involved in this mess. Deepak was as old as I was, perhaps older. Radhika was at least a dozen years younger than him. It didn't seem right to me. And as much as I wanted to, I couldn't simply walk away from the situation.

"Sharad, please help us," Deepak implored.

"What is your plan? You must have thought of something?"

"Yes, we will have a religious ceremony."

"I can't help you with that," I said. "I know nothing about religion or rituals."

"We will find out together."

Deepak said he and Radhika would come to meet me at my workplace to talk about their plan. I agreed reluctantly, but I needed time to think. We walked back together. I left him at his doorstep, and as he was about to open his door, I asked, "Isn't it too soon after your father's death?"

"Well, now we have a place in our home. All these years, my parents had the bedroom. Now, my mother will move into the living room. So I can take the bedroom. You know how it is. You are going to face the same problem when you decide to get married. There is no space. Our homes are too small. But my mother doesn't know about Radhika yet."

The situation was messier than I had imagined, but Deepak had a Zen-like calmness.

Deepak brought Radhika to my workplace the following week. She was wearing a bright yellow kurta and blue jeans, and he was in his regular white shirt and royal-blue trousers. They seemed content, happy, and it seemed that the only thing that mattered to them was that they were together. I was meeting Radhika again after a long time; although we all lived in Teli Gali, our paths no longer crossed. She had grown into a fine young woman. I felt protective of her and couldn't help feeling annoyed at Deepak. I took them to the Irani café for tea and bun maska.

"You will have to plan a trip to Dabhol," Deepak said.

I looked at him incomprehensibly. "Where is that?" Little did I know then that this sleepy town, more like an overgrown village, would in the next couple of years become the centre of a raging global controversy over a power plant, and a multinational company called Enron.

"It is not too far from Ratnagiri. Radhika's maternal uncle has a home there. He will help us get married," Deepak said. Radhika nodded earnestly. "He has arranged for a priest at the local temple to perform the rituals," she said.

"And why is he willing to help? Does he not know that you are not an adult and can't be legally married?"

Both Radhika and Deepak frowned at me. "I am just six months short of eighteen. I am not willing to accept that the state can set an arbitrary age that determines when I should or can get married," Radhika said.

I wasn't expecting a polemical response and looked at her with renewed interest, and before I could ask, "What do you mean?" she said, "If you know your history, you will know that the state has arbitrarily changed the minimum age of marriage for women. A century and more back, it was raised to twelve years. Now, you tell me, if a girl could be married at twelve in the late nineteenth century, why can't she be married at seventeen in the late twentieth century." She looked at Deepak for approval.

"Don't argue with her, she will defeat you with facts," he said. "She is planning to do her PhD in history after she completes her master's. She knows everything about everything."

He looked at her with a mixture of affection and pride.

"No, no, Dipu, don't exaggerate. Not everything, just a few specific historical facts," Radhika said. I was incredulous, she was treating him like a child.

Now, with the preliminaries behind us, we got down to specifics. We would be hiring a car and going to Dabhol next weekend. We would stay at Radhika's uncle's place, and from there, we would go to a temple for the ceremony. I still wasn't sure why they needed me when everything seemed to have been worked out.

"You are our backup. If something doesn't go as planned, you will have to jump in to resolve it. After all, you are a journalist. You can deal with anything," Deepak said.

I was amused at his naivety but didn't want to disappoint them. Looking at them together, in such a perfect state of bliss, I began to convince myself that this wasn't as dreadful as it had seemed initially. I mean, both Deepak and Radhika were committed to their future, and if I could be a catalyst in making them into a married couple, it couldn't be wrong; except, of course, that niggling fact that she was at least a dozen years younger than he.

The following weekend, we got into a swanky new red Maruti. The driver, Bidhan, was also the owner.

We began the journey early in the morning. Deepak came to pick me up, and we drove to Andheri railway station to pick up Radhika. She had informed her parents that she was going on a trip with her classmates to conduct field research. I wondered how gullible her parents had to be to believe such an obvious lie. But then, Suresh Mama and his wife Pragnya were simple people. Suresh Mama was popular in Teli Gali, he was everyone's maternal uncle. Every year, on India's Republic Day, he organized a song and dance competition for children and gave away cakes as the prizes.

I sat next to Bidhan, who reeked of some unknown brand of perfume. The red Maruti breezed past the thin morning traffic. The day was still young, the sun just a nebulous ochre orb. In a couple of hours, it would turn on its tropical ferocity and become unbearable.

I had borrowed a novel from the Lokmanya Seva Sangh library

in Vile Parle to read on the trip. Radhika and Deepak were engrossed in deep conversation. She was telling Deepak her parents' reaction to her story about going on a field trip. "They were so impressed. I told them that we are going to the Ratnadurg fort," she said, and giggled.

We reached Dabhol in the afternoon. It looked like an idyllic village, still in the nineteenth century. Radhika guided Bidhan to her uncle Dinkar's house. He was waiting outside. He waved hesitantly at the car with one hand, while holding the other up to shield his eyes from the sun. Radhika rushed out and leaped into his arms. Dinkar seemed reserved in his reciprocating. Deepak got out of the car and walked to him, bowing to touch his feet, surprising Dinkar, who immediately pulled him up. Radhika introduced Bidhan and me to her uncle; he smiled slightly and led us inside the house.

A group of men on the verandah got up from their chairs and greeted us with folded hands. Dinkar led us through the door.

The house was a decrepit two-storied wooden structure. The rooms were dark, and although the village had electricity, there was no power here. Dinkar's wife, Pushpa, greeted us as we settled on large wooden chairs covered with soft cushions. Pushpa served us lime juice.

Pushpa suggested we take turns to have a bath. "I have warm water ready for all of you," she said, looking at Radhika.

"I am not sure I want to have a bath, but yes, I don't mind splashing some cold water on my face," Radhika said, and taking a towel from her aunt she headed to the washroom at the back of the house, at the far end of the backyard.

We settled into an awkward silence, slowly sipping the lime juice. Dinkar sat expressionless opposite Deepak. When Radhika returned, she had changed into a comfortable-looking house gown.

"Let us have lunch," Pushpa said, and asked Radhika to get everyone inside.

We walked to the backyard, washed our hands and feet with warm water, and then returned to the kitchen, which was a large room with a separate section for cooking; it had blackened from smoke. Dinkar led us to the section where *thalis* were set on small stools. We sat on the floor, which was covered with a straw mat. Pushpa and Radhika carried copper vessels with freshly cooked pomfret masala, shrimp curry, vegetables, and rice. We helped ourselves to a traditional coastal Maharashtra meal.

After lunch, Dinkar led us back to the living room. He offered us paan, which Bidhan took with unconcealed delight, but both Deepak and I declined. Dinkar then called the group of men who were sitting outside to come in.

"We are ready," he said, looking at the leader of the group, who was a tall, large man.

He walked forward and grabbed Deepak by the hand and began to pull him out of the house, another man helping him, when Deepak, after his momentary surprise, began to shout and struggle. Radhika, who was busy helping her aunt in the kitchen, ran out when she heard the commotion. The other men came and grabbed Bidhan and me. They pushed us out of the house. A police Jeep had suddenly materialized outside Dinkar's house. We were pushed into the vehicle, which sped away, leaving behind a cloud of dust. I saw Radhika jostling with her aunt, who was holding her back from running behind the vehicle.

After a brief ride, the Jeep stopped at a police station. We were pushed inside. An officer dressed immaculately in starched uniform walked up to us and motioned for us to sit down on a bench.

"You are all under arrest," he said in Marathi.

"What for?" Deepak asked.

"For forcing a minor to get married . . . "

"That is absurd," Deepak said, but was silenced by a hard slap across his face, delivered with a combination of ferocity and utter delight by the officer.

"Don't act smart with me. I am Inspector Vikram Bhalerao." He instructed the police constables who had brought us to the station to take us to the lockup. We were shoved into a small room smelling of urine and littered with beedi stubs. There was no bench here and so we sat on the floor. The right side of Deepak's face had turned crimson and was swollen, Vikram Bhalerao's fingermarks visible.

Bidhan began to shout, "I just drove the car! I didn't even know why they were coming here." Bhalerao walked up and tried to slap Bidhan, who swiftly moved away and shouted, "Don't you dare touch me! I will get Vasant Saraf."

Bhalerao looked at Bidhan with respect when he heard the name of Bombay's police commissioner. After weighing the situation and a moment's hesitation, he said, "Okay, you go."

"I will come back," Bidhan said.

Deepak was still nursing his right cheek. "If anyone asks, tell them that Radhika was on a field trip to the fort near Ratnagiri. We just accompanied her because we were coming this way."

Bidhan nodded and quickly left.

I was too dazed and scared to react. I should have trusted my instincts. I didn't have a good feeling about it from the time Deepak told me about his plan. For the next six hours we sat silently on the floor of that dingy lockup. There was nothing to talk about. Periodically, Deepak would apologize. "I am sorry, Sharad. I shouldn't have involved you in all this."

"If you were sure that Radhika's uncle was going to help you, why did you even need me?"

"You were to be our backup; in case something went wrong."

"Well, I am in no position to help you, now that things have gone completely wrong."

"No, Bidhan will work something out. He is resourceful. He knows people."

It was late in the evening when Bidhan returned, accompanied by a lawyer. The lawyer had signed bail papers for both Deepak and me, and Bhalerao, who was getting ready to go home, accepted the bail papers without demur and let us off.

When Deepak offered him a bribe, Bhalerao felt insulted and shouted, "Do you want one on the other cheek?" I pushed Deepak away to the door.

Bidhan led us to his car outside and told us what he had done in those six hours. "First, I drove to Ratnagiri. I went to the local Shiv Sena office and asked the person there to help me connect with Sitaram Dada." Sitaram Dalvi was the local legislator from Teli Gali, a gangster turned politician. He had run several illicit hooch distilleries for many years but had given that up to become a builder.

Bidhan had given a car and a driver to Sitaram when he turned into a politician, and Sitaram had not forgotten that gesture. On Sitaram's instructions, Bidhan went to a local lawyer, Kailash Rajawade, and got the bail plea drafted. Then he drove back to Dabhol with the lawyer and got us released on bail. It was a simple, straightforward use of political connections. The lawyer reiterated that we had offered Radhika a ride to Ratnagiri and Dabhol.

Bidhan drove to Dinkar's house, and as he parked the car, he turned to Deepak and said, "Go, get her."

Deepak got out of the car and purposefully went inside. He returned looking crestfallen. "She has already left for Bombay with her uncle," he said.

We reached Bombay past midnight. I got home and went to bed. The next day I had my regular shift and went to work. It was late in the evening when I met Deepak, who was waiting for me at the entrance to the Teli Gali park.

"Look, I am sorry for what happened," he said.

"No, no, don't bother about me. What is the situation with Radhika?"

"Her parents have agreed. We will wait for six months for her to turn eighteen."

But in six months, Radhika decided that her education was more important and postponed her wedding plans indefinitely. Eventually they got married after she had completed her PhD and had secured a job at the Kalina College campus.

Teacher

The invitation was a plain, typed letter, delivered to the tabloid's office and addressed to the editor, who, without a second glance, passed it on to the chief reporter, who was about to throw it into the bin when I pounced on it. It was from a civil liberties organization. A trip was being planned for Bombay journalists to visit Manibeli, a village that would be among the first to be submerged by the construction of the Sardar Sarovar dam on the Narmada River.

The dam was to be the biggest of the many dams in a project that would—on paper—transform Madhya Pradesh, Maharashtra, and Gujarat, the three Indian states through which the Narmada River flowed. Sanjana, an activist friend, had already informed me about the protest, which was organized by the Narmada Bachao Andolan (Agitation to Save the Narmada). I was keen to go and report, but I also knew that the tabloid's management and editorial decision makers would not be in favour.

I had told our chief reporter about the agitation. The inscrutable GV Soni, or GVS, as he was universally known, immediately responded, "The Narmada Bachao Andolan is against development." He peered at me through his reading glasses, frowned, sighed, and asked, "Should we be giving space to it?"

"Yes," I said. "This agitation in Manibeli is a follow-up to Medha Patkar's twenty-two-day hunger strike of last year. Patkar is the voice of the voiceless Adivasis agitating against the dams. She was trying to convince the world that these people were being swindled out of their rights."

"After Rajiv Gandhi's assassination, Indians are looking for unity, not schisms," GVS said. "There is no support for this sort of agitation right now." He was right. A new government would take India on a different economic path that worshiped market forces and had little patience for the Adivasis.

But I knew that GVS supported the environmental cause. He had become a journalist in the late 1950s and believed in Jawaharlal Nehru's ideal of an inclusive India. Subsequently, he had supported Indira Gandhi throughout her political career, except during the Emergency. The horror of Rajiv Gandhi's assassination just a couple of months ago was fresh in his mind, and, for whatever it was worth, Rajiv Gandhi had exhibited the same concerns about the environment as his mother.

But I realized that I wouldn't be able to convince GVS, and so I suggested that he should talk to Sanjana. He agreed immediately. He liked Sanjana; she was a rising star. They were on the same side but the difference between GVS's generation and Sanjana's generation of activists was that the former equated environmental protection with protecting forests, while the latter focused on the rights of the forest-dwelling Adivasis, who would be displaced by mega projects.

At the meeting, Franklin accompanied Sanjana. As always, she wore jeans and bright cotton kurtas, and smelled of expensive perfume; Franklin wore a lawyer's uniform—a white shirt and trousers and a black jacket. There was the shine of Brylcreem on his hair; like GVS, Franklin had stained teeth, but he smiled more easily and longer.

"These are the temples of modern India," GVS said.

"Your notion of development is three decades old," Sanjana said.

"Your notions are fanciful, they benefit nobody and only prevent economic development," GVS said in exasperation.

"No. The dam will turn a majestic river into tiny rivulets. The environmental and ecological damage will be incalculable," Sanjana retorted.

He looked at her patiently. But Sanjana wasn't done yet. She went on, her voice raised, "The project is too ambitious and costly and is unlikely to ever be completed. It will destroy acres of natural forests, harm the delicate and fragile ecological balance, and displace thousands of Adivasis, whose traditional lands will be submerged, and who will be deprived of their livelihood."

That got GVS's attention: destruction of forests, turning a mighty river into tiny rivulets. He agreed—reluctantly—that I could represent the tabloid to cover the Manibeli agitation. "But I doubt if the management will agree to pay for the trip," he said. Sanjana offered to pay.

I would accompany Sanjana and Franklin, who would take the train to Dhule and then a Jeep to reach Manibeli. They were too well known to risk being in a group; if spotted they would likely be arrested under the draconian National Security Act in force in the entire valley. It gave sweeping powers to the state governments to arrest activists.

To avoid detection we took the Amritsar Express from Bombay to Dhule. We reached Dhule early next morning, I alighted from the train with a twinge of regret that my first trip in a first-class compartment had been so brief and I had slept through it.

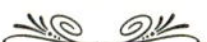

Franklin had reserved two rooms in a hotel and arranged for a pickup from the railway station. Jaffarbhai, the owner and driver of the Jeep, would be with us for the duration of the trip. He would take us to Manibeli later that afternoon. He wore a brown Pathan suit, had coloured his hair and beard with henna, smelled of *itar*, and had a red mouth full of paan that he chewed with single-minded focus, frequently letting out a stream of red expectorate.

He had the appearance of a wizened *fakir*—large ears, long, beaky nose, narrow eyes; but more pertinently, he had the patience of a philosopher. Expertly, without losing temper, he navigated the narrow, congested roads of Dhule, where the traffic was simply anarchic, everyone following their own rules. Dhule was then a one-street town, and like many places in India, three centuries coexisted on its streets, with carts pulled by animals, horse-driven tongas, too many two-wheelers, autorickshaws, state transport buses, swanky SUVs, Ambassadors, Fiats, and Marutis.

The hotel looked derelict from the outside but was magnificent inside. Only the name of the hotel—Taj Palace—was derivative; everything else about it was authentic. The single-storied wooden building was vintage nineteenth century. It reminded me of the guesthouse in the Bahedi sugar factory, where I had worked previously. The staff wore navy-blue uniforms, including blue Gandhi caps. One of the attendants took me to my room.

Everything—the room itself, the bed, the chair, the two chandeliers, and the fan on the ceiling—seemed two sizes larger than anything in a similar hotel in Bombay. The attendant gave me the keys to the room and to the wooden almirah. He left after I tipped him. I had a shower in a well-furnished, well-maintained bathroom. It did not have a commode, but there were two separate sections next to it, marked WC and Smoking Room. The hotel was truly vintage.

I went down to the dining room for breakfast; it, too, in its opulence reminded me of the guesthouse at the Bahedi sugar factory. Sanjana and Franklin were already there, waiting to be served their tea.

"Let's not wait for lunch. We will leave after breakfast; we should be in Manibeli by late evening," Sanjana said, and Franklin and I nodded.

Jaffarbhai was ready. We got into his Jeep after breakfast and began our journey to Manibeli. With the dexterity he had exhibited previously, he pulled onto the highway and then dangerously increased speed. The Jeep didn't need an air conditioner because the front section was doorless. The wind tore in, making it difficult to breathe normally.

"Close the open section or reduce your speed!" Sanjana shouted.

"It is a six-hour journey, we can't be slow, otherwise we will be driving through the forest at night," Jaffarbhai said. He stopped and pulled out two makeshift doors from beneath the back seats, attached them to each side of the Jeep, and again lunged onto the highway at maniacal speed.

"We will have lunch at the Dharamchand Govardhanram Hotel, which is about halfway to Manibeli," he said. "It is vegetarian."

"We would prefer nonvegetarian," Sanjana said. "And I am sure, so would you."

Jaffarbhai looked at her from the rear-view mirror and gave a laugh.

We were passing through one of the least developed areas of India, the home of the Adivasis; occasionally we would pass a village, but mostly it was dense forest on both sides of the highway. Milestones passed swiftly by, as did the trees lining the highway, brown at the base and with a white stripe in the middle. We reached the Dharamchand Govardhanram Hotel ahead of time; what we had gained was about to be squandered because Jaffarbhai discovered that his Jeep had developed a problem.

"So, what? It won't start at all?" Sanjana asked.

"No. It will start, but we may come to a sudden stop in the middle of nowhere. It would be better if we looked for another vehicle," Jaffarbhai said, scratching his beard and peering into the vehicle's hood. He walked back to the hotel and spoke to the man at the cash counter. After a brief chat, he returned.

"Dharamchand babu is the local MLA. He is here and will be leaving for Gaman, a town on the way to Manibeli. He is usually accompanied by a convoy. We should find a place for you three in one of the vehicles," Jaffarbhai said.

Dharamchand Govardhanram Rajawat was a Marwari whose ancestors had moved from Rajasthan to settle in Dhule. The joint family lived together in a mansion. For three generations they had run trade and commerce in the region, and Dharamchand became the first MLA of the Bharatiya Janata Party (BJP). He was delighted that Sanjana would accompany him to Gaman, a typical rural Indian elite enamoured by the urban Indian elite. He greeted us amiably with folded hands and spoke in Hindi.

"We will leave soon. You may come with me in my car," he said to Sanjana, but she declined, saying she would prefer to be with us. He immediately turned to speak to the driver of his Ambassador and told him to arrange for another Ambassador for the three of us. He spoke in a local dialect that was a combination of Marathi and Gujarati with a smattering of Marwadi.

"You will have to stay at Gaman overnight," Jaffarbhai told us.

"Where will we stay?"

"You can stay overnight at our bungalow, or the government *dak* bungalow," Dharamchand said.

"We will stay at the government guesthouse," Franklin said.

Dharamchand nodded.

Jaffarbhai would stay at the Dharamchand Govardhanram Hotel and follow us to Manibeli when his Jeep got repaired.

We reached Gaman late in the evening and stopped at the government *dak* bungalow, alongside the highway on the outskirts of the town. The staff at the bungalow saluted and bowed to Dharamchand. He walked straight to the manager's room and knocked on the door. A groggy-eyed man, wearing a vest and pyjamas, opened the door and bowed to him with folded hands.

"Tadvi, ask your cook to prepare a meal for three, make it mutton. These are guests all the way from Bombay. Look after them. They will leave for Manibeli tomorrow morning. Make them proper masala tea with milk in the morning when they get up and serve them eggs and toast with butter and jam for breakfast. No effort is to be spared. There is a journalist in the team."

Dharamchand returned to his car and Tadvi took us to our rooms which, though sparsely furnished, were well maintained. Each room had a bed covered in a mosquito net and a wooden rack. Although it was late, we decided to sit in the lounge before dinner. The area was covered under a large net to prevent mosquitos and other insects from entering the bungalow. As we settled down, Tadvi brought a bottle of local whisky and beer and glasses with ice. He also served fresh onion pakoras.

"Dinner in an hour," he said.

Sanjana invited Tadvi to join us, and he politely declined. But when Franklin insisted, and almost pulled him down to an empty chair, he folded his hands. "Saab ji, can I invite a person who is also in the guest house?"

"Yes, of course, please do so immediately," Sanjana said.

"Who is he?" I asked.

"He is a schoolteacher. He teaches at the government primary school."

"Go, get him," I said.

Tadvi went and returned with a heavyset man in a white kurta-pyjama. He sat down beside me.

"Saab ji, this is our teacher, Prakash," Tadvi said.

Prakash greeted us with a smile and folded hands. Tadvi handed him a glass of whisky, which Prakash grabbed with a look of pleasure.

"Cheers!" he said as he gulped down the whisky. "Fill it up," he said, looking at Tadvi, and then turning to Franklin, said, "It has been a while," speaking first in Marathi then switching to English. "You are from Bombay?"

"Yes," Sanjana said.

"Dalsukh told me you are all going to Manibeli," Prakash said, now looking at Sanjana, and then at Franklin. He couldn't make out who was the leader of our group. He ignored me altogether.

"Yes, we are going to see the protest against the dam," Franklin said.

"Not just see, also participate," Sanjana said.

"Who is Dalsukh?" I asked.

Tadvi came accompanied by two boys carrying trays of food.

"Saab ji, my name is Dalsukh. Tadvi is my *jaati*. Dharamchand babu calls me by that name—Tadvi," he said, and smiled, as he placed the food on the table.

"Dalsukh, why don't we have dinner in the dining room," Prakash said. "It will be more relaxing. We can switch on the fans using the generator."

"Okay, Masterji, I will take it in," Tadvi said. He turned and nodded at the boys to go inside. I noticed respect in his voice, and even his demeanour was submissive.

We sat for nearly an hour before going to the dining room; during that time Prakash drank a lot of whisky.

"I will give you ten thousand rupees," Prakash said, looking at Franklin, and then at Sanjana. "You help me get out of this town."

Tadvi, who was carefully arranging the food on the dining table, looked at Prakash with curiosity. He didn't follow what Prakash had just said, but from the looks on our faces, he guessed.

"Masterji, please don't get me into trouble," he said, speaking slowly. "I requested that our guests invite you to join them for dinner because you have not had such a grand meal since you came here."

"Dalsukh, I don't care about your *khana-peena*. I want my freedom," Prakash said, speaking in Marathi, sounding at once angry and distressed. "You have imprisoned me here."

"What is going on here?" Sanjana asked, looking both worried and exasperated.

"Madam, this is a jail for me," Prakash said, his voice rising. He pushed back his hair and tried to get up but slumped back into the chair.

"What do you mean? Why?"

"He is just drunk," Franklin said.

"Yes, I am drunk, but I am also in jail," Prakash said.

"Are you being kept here against your will?" Sanjana asked.

"Ask him," Prakash said, pointing at Tadvi.

Tadvi asked the boys to leave the room. They also locked the door from outside, and stood next to the window, watching the drama unfolding inside.

"I am in jail," Prakash shouted, then suddenly ripped off his shirt, and began to wail.

We turned to Tadvi for explanation, but none was forthcoming.

He just stood there trying to calm Prakash. "Masterji, *meharbaani kara*. Please stop this now."

But Tadvi's cajoling just made Prakash angrier. He suddenly rushed to the dining table and grabbed a fork, and tried to plunge it in his chest, and when it didn't get him the desired result, he began to bang his head hard on the table and then ran to the wall and banged it so hard that he fell on the floor. Blood oozed from his nose and mouth, and he continued to wail and beat his head with his hands, even as Tadvi rushed to him and tried to help him get up.

Franklin walked up to Tadvi and told him to call Dharamchand immediately. Tadvi shook his head and raised his hands to convey that it wouldn't be the right thing to do. But Sanjana, too, looked anxious and worried.

"We must get help. Otherwise, this man will harm either himself or us," she said.

Tadvi reluctantly asked the boys to unlock the door. As soon as they did, Prakash sprang up on his feet and ran out.

Before any of us could reach him, an oncoming truck ran over him, killing him instantly.

Dharamchand didn't answer his phone. His orderly told Tadvi that the Saab was asleep and couldn't be disturbed. Sanjana grabbed the phone from his hand and shrieked, "You better inform him, or we are coming there."

Dharamchand's secretary came on the line and said he would send help. A group of men came to the accident site almost immediately. Two police constables accompanied them. Together they lifted Prakash's body from under the truck and put it inside an ambulance. Dharamchand asked Tadvi and the bystanders who had gathered to get buckets of water. They poured water on the road to wash away the blood. Then, the ambulance and the police drove away.

The truck driver was asked to take his vehicle to the police station. He was assured that he would be let off soon, as the accident wasn't his fault. In less than an hour, everything was back to normal; nobody could have guessed that a man had lost his life on the road.

We stood outside the dak bungalow. Sanjana was sobbing, Franklin comforted her. Tadvi stood rooted to the spot outside the gate, quiet, without any expression. I asked him to come inside. He nodded and accompanied me.

"Why was he kept here against his will?" Sanjana asked Tadvi when we were inside.

Tadvi sighed loudly and then spoke without emotion. "Madam, he was appointed as a schoolteacher three months ago. Our village is a punishment posting. Nobody wants to come here and teach. We have seen many teachers come and go. Our children don't get the education they should get because no teacher wants to teach Adivasi children.

When Prakash came here from Nasik, he wanted to go back, feigning illness. But the villagers had become wise to this ploy and decided to keep him in the guest house and not let him leave. He would get the best treatment the village could afford—food, drinks, women. He would be accompanied every morning to the school, teach there, and then be brought back to the guest house. The men of the village took turns to keep a watch on him."

Tadvi looked at us and continued, "I cooked the best food for him every day. Better than what he would have had where he came from. We even arranged for a woman to spend time with him. But he wasn't interested. He had whisky once a week, but he wanted to return to his wife and his young daughter in Nasik. Now they will never see him."

Plague

I saw her when I opened my eyes. She was on the bed next to mine, in a hospital ward; there was an overpowering smell of disinfectants in the room. Her nose—shaped like a hook—and her brown eyes were the most striking parts of her face. The bandage on her forehead was smeared with blood above her left eye.

Her green salwar kameez had a Hawaiian floral pattern. She smiled uncertainly; unsure if it was the right thing to do when people around us were dying. Doctors and nurses ran around trying to bring order to the mounting chaos in the hospital ward as more victims were being brought in.

The police must have brought me to the hospital. I had passed out when I was thrown off the bus when the bomb went off at Worli. People around me had turned into mangled heaps of ripped flesh and shredded bones. Thick black smoke had engulfed the bus. I gagged on the nauseating smell of burning flesh and tar; it would stay with me forever. My clothes were soaked in blood, not all of it was mine. I don't know how, but I survived.

"Were you on the bus, too?" I asked her, trying to sound friendly but not succeeding.

"No, I was walking on the pavement," she said.

From the two nurses, who were cleansing wounds of a victim on another bed, I learnt that thirteen bombs had ripped through the city. I sat up on the bed. This was serious. I would have to call my newspaper.

I looked at my hands and arms, raising my legs a bit; my clothes were in bloody tatters, I was sore in the back and my arms and knees were bruised, but I hadn't broken any bones. I got up from the bed and slowly took a few steps. I decided I didn't need medical attention and was unlikely to get any even if I needed it because the hospital ward was teeming with people who were more seriously injured.

"I am leaving," I said, looking at her.

"I should, too," she said.

"Are you all right?"

"Yes, I am fine. I just have stomach pain. My home isn't far from here. I am at Carter Road," she said.

I called my news desk from the public phone in the lobby. The news editor told me to return to work. I wasn't keen to do that, but he insisted I return because Bombay hadn't seen anything like this before, and the tabloid would need everyone.

We left the hospital together and got into an autorickshaw waiting outside. The traffic on the street was surprisingly thin.

"Pehle Carter Road, *aur udhar se Andheri*," I told the rickshaw driver.

"I will have to go home. Dadi would be worried." I said to myself. I noticed her nod. "I am Sharad," I said.

"Nupur."

"I am a journalist. I work for *Morning Star*. I was returning home in the bus when the bomb exploded," I said.

"I know," she said, and smiled.

"Which part?"

"I saw you at the *Morning Star* when I was interviewed last week. You looked familiar and I was trying to remember where I had seen you but couldn't."

"You must have met Cyrus."

"Yes."

I was surprised to learn this from Nupur. I had only recently quit the *Evening Standard* and moved to the *Morning Star* on a promotion. I was offered the Chief Reporter's post, which I readily accepted. I had worked long enough with the legendary GVS and now needed to move on and up. Cyrus Modi was the editor. Everyone generally disliked him, and nobody more than me.

Not sure where my chat with Nupur would lead, I became quiet and looked outside. She smiled when she got off, and briskly walked away to her building.

My Dadi panicked when she saw my bloodstained shirt.

"It isn't my blood. I helped an accident victim," I lied. Dadi would have had a heart attack if I told her that I was in the bus that blew up.

After chai, I left for work again. Trains were on time and the streets bustled as always. It didn't seem like Bombay had been battered by one of the world's worst terror attacks; and as I learnt later when I reached the tabloid office, more than three hundred people had died within the span of half an hour.

At the paper, the reporting department was buzzing with excitement; everyone had theories for the cause of the serial bomb blasts. I didn't tell anyone that I was in the bus that blew up, not wanting to be the centre of attention. At that moment, I was more annoyed that I would miss my weekly day off. Cyrus summoned me.

"Our coverage must be better than the others," he said.

"It will be, we have a talented team," I said. This was my routine response to Cyrus's attempt to create hype. Everyone knew we were among the lowest paid journalists in Bombay. I had taken the job because the title was a promotion, not because of my new salary.

"After all this bomb business is over, I want you to handle the features sections in addition to your present responsibility," he said.

"But Cyrus, I can barely manage reporting. You should pay me more," I said.

"We are hiring fresh staff," he said impatiently. He told me of Nupur's impending appointment and then dismissed me with a wave of his hand.

A couple of days later, when I was on the day shift, Nupur came for her final interview. She was in a pink linen kameez and a white salwar and went into Cyrus's office. About fifteen minutes later, they walked out, smiling. Cyrus introduced her to the staff. Then he came to my desk.

"This is Sharad. You will be working with him," he said, looking first at her and then at me.

"Nupur is joining us from tomorrow."

"We have met," she said, and shook my hand.

"Not recently," I quickly said.

Nupur looked at me with a raised eyebrow.

"Sharad will tell you what to do," Cyrus said. He wanted to know more but couldn't ask and walked away slowly.

"Why did you lie?" she asked when Cyrus had returned to his office.

"I haven't told anyone I was at the hospital," I said.

Nupur was an eager learner; that evening we went home together in a cab.

"I can't commute by train, I have chronic stomach pain," she said.

During the cab ride, she wouldn't stop asking personal questions. She wanted to know about my family. I told her I lived with my Dadi and my sister Neeta, and I told her about my father's suicide and my mother's mental condition.

She told me about Anand Vanmali, her dad; her mother had died when she was young. "What is your mother's name?" she asked.

"Prameela. She has dementia. She is in a sanatorium in Khandala."

When I reached home, Dadi was sitting by the kitchen window on her wooden chair, watching the traffic and fanning herself desultorily. She looked at me as if she was seeing a ghost.

"No booze today?" she asked, and chuckled.

I ignored her. I switched on the fan and went to have a shower. Then I served myself dinner. It was the same everyday—rice and dal. My silence irritated her.

"What is the matter, why are you home so early?"

"Do you want me to go back and return later?"

She glowered at me and returned to scrutinizing the traffic. After dinner I tried to sleep early but couldn't and lay awake thinking of Nupur.

Over the next few months, Nupur and I turned from colleagues into friends. Our work and our schedules kept us together. We went to the local Irani café for lunch, and we went home together in a cab. One day after our lunch, she pulled out a box from her bag.

"Give me your hand," she said.

She put a pastry in my palm.

"I love you," she said, and giggled nervously.

I gaped at her.

"You have nothing to say?" she asked, her smile quickly vanishing; tears welled up in her eyes.

I was sweating. The café had suddenly become more humid than usual, and everything seemed quiet.

"Why this sudden confession?" I mumbled.

"We are no longer colleagues, and I think we are more than just friends."

"But love . . . ?"

"It is love; you know it as well as I do. I told Dad about us. He wants to meet you."

"We hardly know each other," I said.

"He is expecting you home this evening," she said, sounding anxious; she wasn't even listening to me.

Anand Vanmali was a cheerful man, the kind who causes acute discomfort in others by their general affability.

"Have dinner with us," he said, as he shook my hand. "How is your stomach?" he turned to Nupur with concern.

"Better. No ache today," she said as she went to the kitchen.

"Nupur tells me that you work together, and you have grown quite close," he said, then pointed me towards the couch.

I nodded and sat beside him.

"Are you serious about her?" he asked.

I didn't know what to say, glanced at him nervously, and then looked around the living room.

"She is serious about you, otherwise she wouldn't have told me."

"Nupur hardly knows me," I said.

"If you are together, she will have the time to know all about you," he said.

Nupur wanted to do different things as a journalist and began to take on reporting assignments that took her out of the city. One

September evening, about a year after I first met her, our lives changed permanently.

"Your sister's husband called from Surat; Neeta's in hospital—she has the plague," Dadi told me when I reached home from work.

"This is the 1990s. Nobody has the plague," I said.

"That is what he said. He wants you to call him. It's an emergency. Bal said Neeta is very sick, she may die."

We didn't have a phone at home, which was unusual, but with just Dadi and me at home, it wasn't a necessity, and there was a telephone booth in the street below. Long-distance phone calls were a bother at night because everyone wanted to take advantage of the cheaper rates. I went out and joined the queue at the telephone booth below our home. I spoke briefly to Bal, and he confirmed what Dadi had told me. He sounded tired. I agreed to go to Surat the next morning and help him move his family temporarily to Bombay. Then I called and told Nupur about my plan.

"I am coming with you. I will talk to Cyrus. I will file news reports," she said. She didn't wait for me to agree. Early the next morning, I called Cyrus from the train terminus, only to discover that Nupur had already spoken to him, and he had heartily approved her plans. I was waiting at the ticket counter when she entered the terminus, guileless about the effect she was having on everyone around her.

"You are going to Surat, not Paris," I said, looking at her.

"Oh, shut up. I am not feeling good. My stomach hurts."

"You shouldn't have come."

"And miss this opportunity? No way. Cyrus said I could report for Associated Press. He knows the India bureau chief; that would be my first international assignment."

We reached Surat in the afternoon and checked into a hotel. The hotel manager was not convinced we had a genuine reason to be in the city.

"Everyone who can is leaving," he said.

Surat was dirtier than I had imagined. The autorickshaw ride to the hospital was short but terrifying, because the driver was either high, drunk, or just didn't have any notions of road safety. The hospital looked desolate, and Neeta lay on a filthy bed, with tubes in her nose and her arms. She looked emaciated and shrunken, but smiled weakly when she saw me.

We were meeting again after many years. I didn't know what to say, but she couldn't stop talking.

"Bal should be coming any minute now. He had to go to work to complete some urgent tasks. He will get the two other kids from home; this is the youngest," Neeta pointed at the toddler sitting on the floor, busy with her dolls. "She can't be without me," she said.

I sat beside her and held her hand. She tried to smile, looked at me and then at Nupur.

"This is Nupur," I said. "She works with me. She is here to report on the plague."

Neeta looked at her blankly. Nupur went looking for someone to talk to.

"Have you seen Ma," Neeta asked.

I hadn't seen Ma in a long time. She was in what I called a happy space—unconnected to the real world. The last time I visited her, she flung her bedpan at me. It wasn't empty. The assistants who came to take me away from the room said she didn't recognize anyone.

Bal reached the hospital with the other kids. I had forgotten their names. He greeted me warmly and told me he had heard that the city administration was planning to quarantine the entire city. He had already hired a private cab to take everyone to Bombay, and he told me to inform Dadi that they were coming to Bombay.

"You two shouldn't be here, it's not safe," Neeta said.

"We will be fine, you take care," I said.

In the evening, after Nupur had interviewed some patients, their families, and the municipal officers, we went to the post office to wire her report through the telex machine. She called Cyrus and told him that more than a hundred patients had what doctors believed were plague-like symptoms.

I tried calling the telephone booth below our home to leave a message for Dadi about Bal and Neeta's imminent arrival in Bombay but couldn't get through, and sent a one-line telegram instead: "Neeta-Bal coming to Bombay 27 September." We returned to the hotel. Nupur was exhausted. It had been a busy day. After dinner, she sat by my side and again complained of stomach pain.

"Nupur, what causes these frequent stomach aches?"

"I don't know. I have these sudden attacks on the left side of my stomach," she said. "But they don't last long."

"You should consult a specialist," I said. She nodded absently.

She was waiting for Cyrus's call. He called late at night to tell her that AP had splashed the story across the world. A TV news crew was coming, and the agency wanted Nupur to coordinate. She was excited and wanted to call her dad but decided against it, because he would ask her about me, and she didn't want to lie.

Within a week of its outbreak, the plague in Surat was global news. Nupur was the first local journalist to represent an international wire service. Her dispatches covered all angles—the human tragedy, the administrative lapses, the absence of hygiene, people's resentment over forced quarantine. Her face was on television news across the world. I admired her discipline; she was meticulous and confident. Her transformation was awe-inspiring.

She would be up early, leave the hotel by seven o'clock to visit the hospitals and talk to the medical staff, return for lunch in the afternoon, and leave again for field reporting. By the time she returned, it was dinner time, and often she skipped dinner because she was too tired even to keep awake. She slept peacefully but complained of stomach pain every day. The rigour wasn't doing her any good. Her face was swollen, and she looked tired. Often the pain in her stomach became so severe that she had to stop everything and just lie down. After ten days of such a hectic pace, Nupur fell ill. She was forced to cancel her appointments. I gave her a sedative and a tablet to bring down her fever.

"We must do something about that constant pain in your stomach," I said. "You have been ignoring it for far too long and that won't do you any good."

"I will talk to Dr Kapadia," she said. Dr Rajesh Kapadia was the chief medical superintendent at the same hospital where Neeta was. Nupur and he had become good friends.

"I am worried about the plague," I said, when we met the doctor.

He said, "The evening fever is a symptom of a swelling of the liver. That could be because of both a strain and an infection. It is not the stomach, it is probably Nupur's liver that is the cause of her pain."

He took blood samples for tests and the report confirmed his prognosis. There seemed to be some infection in the liver and a prominent swelling. He touched Nupur over her liver, and she stifled a scream.

"You must take complete bed rest."

"But that is impossible," Nupur said, "I have many deadlines to meet."

Finally, after about three weeks, the media frenzy began to ebb, and we returned to Bombay. I dropped her off at her home and went back to mine. Dadi was up, watching Neeta's kids in bed—the eldest one was still awake; Bal was snoring on the couch. Neeta was on my bed, and she looked better. There was no room for me to lie down. Just as I was about to go to sleep in the kitchen, the guy from the phone booth down below hollered for me. I went to the window.

"Call from Bandra." I ran down to take the call.

"She is in severe pain; I am taking her to a nursing home next door. She is asking for you," Nupur's dad said. He sounded desperate.

"I will be there soon."

"She is on pain killers and sedatives," he told me when he saw me.

I told him about her recurring fever in the evenings in Surat. He didn't hide his irritation.

"You should have told me you were together," he said.

There was no time for recriminations. When I told the doctor on duty about her evening fevers and Dr Kapadia's treatment, he advised that Nupur should be moved to a hospital. I called Cyrus. I had forgotten how late it was. He sounded gruff, but eager to help.

"Take her to Breach Candy, I will make arrangements," he said.

The ambulance sped through the empty roads. Nupur's pain had subsided thanks to the medications. I held her hand. Cyrus had left instructions at the hospital and Nupur was admitted without delay.

Dr Umang Pathak was on duty. He examined her and waited for the blood report.

"Is it serious?" I asked.

He looked at me impassively. "These are classic symptoms of autoimmune hepatitis," he said. "It is a rare ailment. The body's immune system attacks the liver cells and that causes the liver to inflame. It is genetic and afflicts women between the ages of fifteen and forty, and it gets worse swiftly if not treated in time. It may have caused cirrhosis of the liver."

"So it is serious," Nupur's dad said.

"Let us wait and see," Dr Pathak said.

"Nupur must have had these symptoms for some time, but she only complained of pain in her stomach," her dad said, his voice a whisper.

"It is not her stomach; it is liver inflammation that is causing the pain," Dr Pathak reiterated.

"That is what Dr Kapadia also said," I put in.

We waited outside intensive care, exchanging worried glances. A long time later, a nurse came out of the room. She went to Nupur's dad.

"She is still critical," the nurse said.

Finally, Dr Pathak came out. He was candid.

"Nupur's liver has failed," he said. "Unlike the usual cases of liver failure that occur over a long period, this was the rare form where failure occurs within forty-eight hours. There could be multiple causes. The most common cause is the hepatitis virus infection. She is being treated for viral infection. We are hoping that the infection will run its course."

"Will she be okay?" Nupur's dad asked.

Dr Pathak put his hand on his shoulder. "I wish I could say yes. We have tried everything. She is not responding to the treatment," he said.

Nupur's dad was shaken. I had to hold him by his arm. I sat down on the couch, pulled my legs up, and began to cry loudly. The intensive care room remained closed. In the middle of the night, a nurse came to me and said the doctor wanted to see us. We ran. The doctor quietly led us to Nupur's bed.

Her eyes were shut. She was breathing heavily and with difficulty. There were tubes in her nose, her mouth, her wrists, and her stomach. Her dad went and sat beside her. She didn't respond to his touch. I held her hand. She stirred and opened her eyes. She tried to smile, but the effort was painful, and she gasped.

"I love you," I whispered.

She tried to speak, and moved her lips, but she couldn't. Tears rolled down her face. She gripped my hand. Her eyes stayed on me. We looked at each other for a long time. Her heavy breathing turned normal and then slowed. Then it stopped.

The nurse closed Nupur's eyes.

Marriage

I saw Gunjan almost two years after we started exchanging emails. These days it is quite natural for people to meet online and develop an emotional connection before meeting in person, but for us it felt strange to marry a person with whom we had become acquainted through emails.

We weren't total strangers because the emails we wrote to each other were detailed and honest; we were frank about our pasts. When I think about it now, Gunjan helped me heal and overcome the trauma of losing Nupur, while she was trying to get over her failed marriage to Frank and learning to bring up her daughter Aarti.

Dadi insisted that I should not remain single after Nupur passed away and tried to set up meetings with "good girls from good families." But I wasn't willing to abandon the memories of my life with Nupur; she was still a part of me, a large—almost physical—presence in my life. Even if she had ceased to be physically present, she lived on in my mind, and I wanted her to continue living there. I continued to visit her dad every day in the evening initially, and then, at his suggestion, once a week. After a couple of years, he told me that he was selling his home in Bombay and moving to his village, Sinnar, near Poona.

That is when I realized that I too had to move on. I had been living in the past and didn't want to abandon it because I didn't know how. Not unexpectedly, Dadi came to my rescue; she was direct about it. One evening, at dinner, soon after Nupur's dad left Bombay, she gave me a photo of a young woman and her daughter.

"This is Gunjan, with her daughter Aarti. They live in Canada," she said.

"She is young," I said, glancing at the photo.

"But she is a mother, and she is divorced," Dadi said.

"Who is she?"

"Gunjan . . . Chandrakant Mehta's sister."

When she saw the incomprehension on my face, she explained, "Chandrakant is Bal's boss. Gunjan is Chandrakant's sister."

She handed me a piece of paper on which Bal had scribbled an email address and a telephone number. I took it and continued with my dinner while watching the news. A couple of days later, Bal called from Surat to ask if I would consider writing to Gunjan.

"Mr Mehta thinks you two are ideal for each other," he said, without much conviction. From what I could gather, Bal was doing this—getting me hitched up with his boss's sister—only because it would help him in his job.

Bal's several businesses had continued to fail miserably and finally, upon Neeta's insistence, he took up a job at a textile mill, where he seemed to be doing well and had rapidly risen to be the vice-president. Neeta was delighted to be moving in elite circles, to be invited on the weekends to Mr Mehta's mansion; they had even taken a vacation to Singapore. Dadi wasn't sure whether to rejoice, regret, or just be plain annoyed. She could no longer scold Neeta and make her feel guilty for marrying "that brain-dead idiot, that no-good loafer."

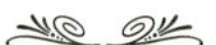

I am not sure why I wrote to Gunjan. Perhaps out of sheer boredom. I had begun to lose interest in my job and my colleagues often hinted that I needed to take time off. I had bought a desktop computer and finally got a telephone line for an internet connection. Once the internet was installed, I discovered a new world. I wrote my first email to Gunjan.

I introduced myself and my family, and she sent me a photograph of her daughter Arty. I reluctantly wrote about Nupur. She responded warmly; she wrote that her brother Chandrakant had already told her about Nupur. She wrote about her failed marriage to Frank, about how they had met at the university and fallen in love and had been married for six years. From Gunjan Mehta she had become Gunjan Mehta-Parker. She had gone to Canada to study biochemistry at the University of Waterloo and then stayed after she found a job. She had lived with Frank in Kitchener and they got married when Arty was born. She moved to Brampton after her separation six months ago. She worked at a branch of a pathological laboratory in Bramalea. Her daughter was four years old.

After a couple of weeks of regular email exchanges, which were detailed, I called her. Gunjan and her daughter were getting ready to leave home—she to work, and Arty to school.

"How are you?" she said, unable to hide the surprise, the excitement in her voice.

"Good," I said. But I didn't have anything to say, and then after an awkward pause, I said, "I wanted to hear your voice."

She giggled, and then said, "Do you like it?"

"Like what?"

"My voice, now that you have heard it."

"Oh yes, yes, of course."

"What time is it in Bombay?" she asked.

"It is ten-thirty at night."

It was clear that both of us were more comfortable writing to each other than talking. In our brief—all too brief—time together, we would become woefully aware of our inability, and later unwillingness, to talk.

"That is late. You should go to sleep."

"Yes, I guess so. I normally sleep around eleven."

I should have asked her about her daughter, I thought later. Gunjan sounded timorous, hesitant. But that could be because she hadn't expected a call from me and was surprised.

The morning after I called Gunjan, she sent me an email.

Hi Sharad,

I must have come across as a cold, disinterested person when we spoke today. It is just that I wasn't expecting a call from you, and we were in our usual morning rush to reach Aarti's school on time (she prefers to spell her name as Arty). Thank you for making the effort to call me. I appreciate it. Please call over the weekend. I will have more time to talk.

Love

Gunjan.

I printed the email and have preserved it because it was the first time she had used "Love." I responded with a longwinded letter that rambled on about my inability to be articulate on the phone, or for that matter, even in person, and how I admired people who could chat for hours on the phone. She wrote back that I should call her on the weekend, and that she would start my training in the art of telephone conversation.

Gunjan called Saturday morning. It was Friday evening in Brampton. And we spoke for three hours—not about us, but about

Frank and Nupur and Arty and her brother Chandrakant and my Dadi. It was obvious that we both lived in the past, or at least were unwilling to let go of it. But she had been right. I was talking freely to her, as she was to me; that initial inhibition had melted.

Now, in addition to our daily emails, we continued calling each other on the weekends. Our phone chats were turning out to be an extended therapy session for both of us. After about three months of this routine, I asked her to come to India. She agreed immediately and without hesitation. Her brother had been calling her for a long time, but she had resisted. She wasn't ready to get married to just about anyone her brother recommended.

"But that is precisely what you are about to do," I said.

"You are different. Yes, you are different."

"Different doesn't mean good."

"Oh, I know that, but I feel comfortable talking to you," Gunjan said.

I went to Surat to meet Gunjan and Arty, who were to fly down from Toronto. Chandrakant Mehta came to receive me at the station. He was the archetype of a buccaneer business baron. I noticed that his hair was vanishing rapidly and prematurely greying. It looked like he had dyed it at home and was inept at it. His forehead didn't seem to end. His eyes were large and penetrating. His nose was thin, and hair stuck out of his nostrils and his ears. He wore a safari suit. He also wore a strong perfume. "It is Brut," he proclaimed when my nose wrinkled involuntarily as I sat beside him in his black Mercedes.

"I am happy it's working out for both of you," he said.

"You are a journalist," he added after a moment, sounding as if no sane person would willingly want to be a journalist.

I nodded.

"Not many opportunities for a journalist in Canada," he said.

I didn't nod this time, merely looked at him.

"But lots of other opportunities," he said.

I looked out of the car window; it had turned dark suddenly. The traffic moved slowly. There were far too many scooters and motorcycles on the road. The Mercedes stood out, as it was meant to. With each passing moment, I was getting more reasons to dislike Gunjan's brother, and he was probably finding different ways to dislike me. Thankfully for both of us, we reached the hotel, and we quickly said our goodbyes. I went to bed early after a sparse meal.

Bal and Neeta arrived the next morning. Prosperity sat well on my sister. She was plump and looked plumper in a blue chiffon saree. All the plague gloominess was a thing of the past. Bal had the cheerfulness of the clueless or the uncaring; I envied him. Everything that he had probably hoped for in his career was finally coming true.

"Gunjan and her daughter will also be staying in this hotel," Bal said, and then added in what I thought was a conspiratorial tone, "She said she wanted to be in the same hotel."

I nodded, not sure how to respond.

Chandrakant Mehta arrived a short while later and led us to the restaurant for breakfast. We waited for Gunjan and Arty to reach the hotel. They had left Toronto the day before and were flying with a stopover in Qatar. Their flight had landed in Bombay, and they were on their way to Surat in one of Chandrakant Mehta's luxury sedans. It was midafternoon by the time they arrived at the hotel.

Gunjan was exhausted. Arty had just woken up from a long sleep.

"For all his business baron appearance, your brother is unconventional," I said.

"What do you mean?"

"He has booked us both in the same hotel."

"Oh, actually, I had insisted on staying in the hotel, because neither I nor Arty would be able to adjust in my brother's mansion," Gunjan said, and then, as an afterthought, added with a smile, "I had called Chandrakant and told him that I would prefer to be in the same room as you, but he freaked out and would have none of that."

The mother and daughter looked tired and jetlagged but Gunjan was happy to be in India; her daughter was sullen.

"Are we in India or in Surat?" Arty asked.

"Yes, we are in both—Surat is in India. Now have your breakfast," Gunjan said, as she pushed Arty's chair closer to the dining table.

"India smells of poo," Arty declared and refused to touch the breakfast.

I had taken an Indianized version of a Barbie doll for her. She grabbed it from my hand and examined it intently.

"What is she wearing?"

"Arty, you have seen a saree before. I have worn one a few times," Gunjan said, exasperated. "Eat, before your breakfast gets cold."

Arty ignored her mother. "And she has got a red dot on her forehead," Arty said, continuing with her examination.

"That is a bindi," I said.

"Huh?" she said, and looked at me, but then got distracted with the doll's nose ring.

"Ma, you told me body piercing is bad, but look, this doll has pierced her nose," Arty exclaimed.

"Out here, it is okay on the ears and nose, not okay anywhere else," Gunjan said.

"How can something be wrong there and right here?" Arty asked.

Gunjan looked at me and we smiled.

Arty put the doll on the table and fed her the cereal, making chomping sounds. She had a bit of cereal and said with utter finality, "I am tired. I want to go back to bed."

Gunjan wasn't sure whether she wanted to go back to her room. But I nodded in assent, and we left the restaurant. Arty was fast asleep as soon as she hit the bed. We walked to the second room, where I sat on the couch and she on a chair. There was nothing to talk about, and we became awkwardly aware that we were alone with each other physically for the first time. I smiled at her. She smiled back, looking down at her toes and then at me and then again at her toes. After a minute or so, which seemed like forever, she got up.

"I must change into something comfortable," she said. She got up and walked to the open bag on the floor and pulled out a cotton shirt and pants. She went to the bathroom, changed, and came and sat beside me. She smelled of toothpaste. We sat in silence for a moment and then I reached for her hand, and she got up and led me to the bed. I followed without hesitation. I hadn't been with a woman since Nupur.

The following week, we were married in a simple ceremony in which Gunjan's brother and an obscure aunt, and Neeta, Bal, and Dadi, were present. We agreed to have our marriage registered in the court when I reached Canada.

Chandrakant Mehta paid an agent for all the immigration processing work, and it took over a year—and altogether two years since we had exchanged our emails—for me to finally reach Brampton. That time helped me get closer to Arty.

She would now call me in Bombay even when Gunjan was busy, and she would talk endlessly and rapidly about her day at school, her friends ("Sylvie is a bully, Rehan is my best friend, Claudia is . . . no, I am not allowed to use that word"), and of course the weather. Now, in addition to the daily emails, Gunjan would also send snail mail to me every week—a hastily scribbled note, with a drawing from or a photograph or two of Arty. I was their family, and they were waiting for me to be with them.

In May 1997, on a Saturday afternoon, I landed at Pearson Airport and Arty jumped into my arms. Gunjan was crying. It was still cold outside, and they wore light cardigans. I had two bags with me. They were excited as Gunjan drove me to their home in an apartment in Bramalea. It was large by Bombay standards and done up tastefully. The walls had paintings, and although the late afternoon sun was bright, Arty turned on the lights.

They had ordered a takeout dinner, but I just had coffee because I had done nothing else but eat and watch movies during the flight. Gunjan suggested I have a shower and change into freshly laundered home clothes—a pyjama and a shirt; she also had a robe for me, which I didn't wear. Gunjan and Arty had been buying my clothes for me. It was obvious that Gunjan had put in a lot of effort to make me feel at home and simultaneously make me feel special.

The next few days were hectic as I completed all the paperwork related to my immigration and opening a bank account. (I realized to my horror that banks charged money here instead of paying interest.) I read the driver's manual and took the test. Gunjan helped me join a newcomers' settlement program at the local library to become familiar with the job market.

I realized that I had to reinvent myself, since journalism was clearly not a feasible option. I had absolutely no idea what I would be doing. I started working at the local grocery outlet at minimum wage, but I had to work different shifts.

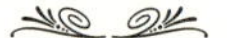

In two months, I had settled in nicely. I called and spoke to Neeta regularly—in fact more regularly than I had done when in India. After I got my first pay, I sent Dadi money, a lot more than her monthly requirement. It was a prolonged process. I couldn't write a letter to her because she couldn't read English, and although I spoke four Indian languages, I could write only in English. Calling her was the only option, and I did that on my weekly offs, using phone cards. After talking to me about what she had done during the week—a routine that she had followed all her life—she would ask me, "Are you happy?"

My response was always the same: "I think so."

She wouldn't say anything more, and we would disconnect.

Then one day she said, "Sharad, you should be sure. If you are not sure it means that you are not happy."

"No, no, Dadi. I am quite happy."

"You always sound hesitant."

My grandmother understood me even when she was thousands of miles away. My hesitancy was due to an unexpected encounter with Frank. He would come over to take Arty with him every alternate weekend, but I was ill-prepared for the continued intimacy that he and Gunjan enjoyed. He was polite with me, but I felt that he adopted a deliberately condescending tone. After our first meeting, I complained to Gunjan, but she answered, "That is how he speaks to everyone. That is how white people speak to non-white people."

I wasn't sure.

"You don't have to talk to him," she said. "He is here for Arty, and he has the court's order to do so. There is nothing we can do about it."

Gunjan was right. Arty was always excited to see Frank. She had a fresh new drawing ready for him every time and would run into his arms and shower him with kisses. Their closeness made me acutely aware that I wasn't ever going to replace him in her life. Arty stayed with Frank in Kitchener every alternate weekend.

Frank was taller than me. His eyes were brown and matched his hair and beard. He almost always wore jeans and a corduroy jacket. He was younger than me and looked like an undergrad student. There was also an easy familiarity between Frank and Gunjan that rankled me. It shouldn't have, considering they had been married.

But it did, and I was jealous. It was the way they exchanged glances and the way they completed each other's sentences, and the way they touched each other spontaneously. I wondered why they had split up, if they could get along so well still.

"Oh, it is over, alright," she said flatly once over breakfast, tears welling up in her eyes. "He left me. He cheated on me."

It was evident to me that she hadn't stopped loving him.

BRAMPTON – TORONTO

Job

It took a couple of years for the newness of Canada to wear thin. The four distinct seasons were a novelty, and winters were longer, much longer, and far colder than I was mentally or physically prepared for, but when you have lived your entire life in the tropics, like I had, the Canadian winter is a beautiful experience. The first snowfall reminded me of Bombay rains. Both, the Bombay rains and the Brampton snow, transform lives.

My new home had its allure and charm, but life and living were not easy. Life is hard, even for those born and raised here, harder for a newcomer. And from what I could make out, it stays hard forever.

For me, the presence of my new family—my wife Gunjan and her daughter Arty—made my transition easier. Or so I thought, until about a year later when the reality of being a newcomer in Canada hit me. It was impossible for me to find a job with my limited skills. Journalists are not equipped to do anything else.

I applied for hundreds of jobs and when nobody wanted me, I reluctantly took a survival position, working at the local Tim Horton's restaurant. It seemed at first like the perfect job, not requiring any skills, but it turned out to be impossibly difficult. Taking a customer's order, and helping to make and deliver it within a couple of minutes, were tasks that required precision and attention. The job was intimidating, and I fumbled ceaselessly during my first few days, before settling into an uncomfortable routine.

But it did offer me my first experience of Canadian multiculturalism—my colleagues were from a variety of ethnicities. Just when I thought I had mastered the impossibly difficult task of handling different machines, I was fired—because I had accidentally put bacon strips into a breakfast sandwich for a Muslim customer, who was brought to tears.

I joined Singh Traders in July 2001.

Rajinder Singh, the owner, was a tall, lean Sikh with a flowing white beard. He had sharp features—a broad forehead, a straight nose, a thin mouth, and baleful eyes that had a strange, mesmerizing effect. He dressed immaculately—invariably in a white shirt, navy blue trousers, a smart jacket, and polished black shoes—and was frugal in his habits. Everyone called him Roger. I decided I was not ever going to call him that and told him that I would address him as Mr Singh. He nodded in approval; he seemed to like it.

Mr Singh followed a set routine every day. He arrived at work at eight-thirty and would be on the telephone for an hour, talking to suppliers or buyers, then attend to paperwork and banking. At ten-thirty he had a cup of Indian masala tea in the office's kitchen and strolled up and down the corridor from the kitchen to his office for about fifteen minutes. At the sides of the corridor were four cubicles for the staff. At noon, Mr Singh stepped out for lunch followed by a brisk walk around the neighbourhood, usually returning with a flyer for some show at the local library or at the Peel Art Gallery Museum that he would visit some evenings after work. He drove an old but well-maintained Honda. He would leave work at four pm every afternoon.

The office was in a stately building in downtown Brampton, close to the Rose Theatre. He had a disciplinarian work ethic that belonged to a world that had long ceased to exist. He expected his staff to share that work ethic. But he was kind-hearted and looked after his people.

A couple of days after I started working, I was so swamped with chores that I had no time to take lunch. On the fourth day he came over to me and said, "The work will never cease, but you should have your lunch and then take a break and go for a walk."

The work itself was monotonous, sleep-inducingly boring; there was nothing exciting or creative about keeping an inventory list and updating orders for a couple of dollars more than minimum wage.

Mr Singh imported household knickknacks from India. The inventory was always expanding. I was shocked at how unyielding Indians were, at their insistence on continuing with their habits and lifestyles. I marveled at the globalization of trade that made it possible for them to continue being Indians thousands of miles away from India.

"You mustn't forget that most of these people who buy the things that your company imports are from the back of the beyond even in India," Gunjan said.

"That may be true, it is just that they don't want to change."

Gunjan nodded without agreeing, and then said, "All of us change, it is inevitable. Life changes us; really, we don't have a choice."

Clearly, we were talking about different things.

My job at Singh Traders helped me contribute to my family's resources. Of course, Gunjan managed the bulk of expenses from her income, and my insistence on a frugal lifestyle helped. I imagined that I had convinced her to save enough money for a down payment on a condo.

Mr Singh continued to pile me with extraordinary amounts of chores, and while he seemed fairly satisfied with my performance, he was completely unwilling to give me even a meagre raise.

"This is routine work; you are overqualified to do it. If you need more money, you should find a job that pays you more. I cannot," he said, without even a moment's hesitation or a trace of guilt, but smiled sweetly.

He intrigued me. His outward appearance made him someone I could relate to—his colour, his turban, his flowing beard. But that was all there was to his Indianness. His detached demeanour, his crisp, impeccable manners, and his accent-free diction revealed his Canadian identity, which was the front and centre of his personality. His inherent decency revealed his rootedness as a human being, and his business acumen was evident in the success of his venture, which he revealed to me was something that he had launched in the late 1980s, soon after he landed in Canada.

I didn't know him well enough to ask him more about his Indian roots, although I was perennially tempted to do so. He told me he preferred to employ new immigrants to help him because he believed in helping newcomers get a start in a new place.

"I was helped too, when I came here. This is how I give back; all immigrants should give back," he said.

I discovered an isolated deli in one of the backstreets of downtown Brampton. In my opinion it had the world's best sandwiches. It didn't have an elaborate menu, just a few options, and one that I had come to love dearly—the modest flatbread egg and cheese sandwich. I had a sandwich and a cup of Columbian coffee at the deli almost every afternoon. It was sumptuous and cheap.

Mr Singh walked into the deli one afternoon, as I sat down with my sandwich. We were surprised to see each other. He asked for my permission to join me at the table, and then walked over with his lunch. "It's shepherd's pie," he said, when I looked at it. I nodded politely, making a mental note that I would have to check with Gunjan what that was.

We didn't exchange a word as we ate. When we were done, he asked me gently, "So, Sharad, what made you come to Canada?"

"I married a Canadian woman," I said.

"Good decision."

"If I may ask you, sir, what made you come here?"

"The situation in Punjab in those days," he said casually, but didn't elaborate.

After a prolonged silence, I hesitantly asked, "Were you personally affected?"

He pulled up the shirt sleeve of his left hand up to the elbow to reveal a nasty scar that ran across the length of his arm.

"They broke my arm. Shattered it, actually."

I gaped at the scar. "I am sorry."

"Don't be. It happened a long time back. It is a bad memory now, nothing more."

We finished lunch and walked back to the office.

"Do you have lunch at the deli every day?"

"Yes. It is affordable and it is delicious."

"I agree. I will see you tomorrow," he said as we climbed the stairs to the office.

He smiled as we entered and then there was an abrupt transformation in his manner—he was back to the detached, aloof employer that he preferred to be.

The question uppermost on my mind was, how was his arm shattered? Was he in any way involved with the militancy that had gripped Punjab in the 1980s? Was he a militant himself?

I was determined to ask him at least the first question, and Mr Singh had anticipated it. The next day, when we met for lunch at the deli, he waited for us to finish and then, without my prompting, he began to narrate his story.

"I joined Khalsa College in Patiala as a professor of political science in 1976. It was a good job. I enjoyed it because I loved teaching and I loved the subject. The students were in their first year in college and enthusiastic but had difficulty accepting a professor who was not much older than them.

"Four years later, I met a girl called Jasmeet who had come in as a first-year student. She was smart and keen to learn. Her father—Balwant Singh—or one of her brothers dropped her off at the college and picked her up in the afternoon. There was a mutual attraction between us, although there was nearly a decade's gap in our age.

"A year later, when she was in her second year, Jasmeet confided in me that her younger brother Joginder—Jogi—had joined the militants. She seemed both apprehensive and excited," Mr Singh said.

"I was in Bombay at that time," I said, "still in college. We weren't sure what was happening in Punjab."

"The situation in Punjab then was a search for identity and justice. It still is. But let me continue with my story," he said, almost pleadingly.

I nodded.

"In about a week, Jasmeet came home with Balwant Singh. The

police had arrested Jogi. The father pleaded with me to help the family."

This was turning out to be a long narrative, and over the next week he completed it.

I learnt that he along with Jasmeet and Balwant Singh went to the police station to inquire about Jogi's whereabouts. There was an altercation at the police station, and the police officer hit Balwant Singh on the head with a cane. Though he was wearing a turban, he was grievously injured, losing consciousness. He had to be rushed to a local hospital.

Mr Singh and Jasmeet were arrested. The police were convinced that they had more information about local militants. Mr Singh was beaten multiple times with a cane. "They broke my arm in different places. I had multiple fractures," Mr Singh said softly, as I gaped at him.

The college administration intervened to get Mr Singh and Jasmeet released, after which they decided to move to Delhi. It was the wrong decision because soon after, Sikh security officers assassinated India's Prime Minister, Indira Gandhi, and Sikhs were systematically targeted in a pogrom that resulted in the infamous 1984 Sikh massacres.

Mr Singh and Jasmeet were at home in Old Delhi in their *barasati*—a single rooftop room with a verandah that overlooked the magnificent Jama Masjid. Two men broke the door and barged in, holding a hatchet and rods. They attacked Mr Singh with the rods, hitting him all over. The arm that had barely begun to heal was dislocated at the shoulder, hanging loose at the joint. The men then took turns to sexually assault Jasmeet, and, when she tried to fight back, hit her with a hatchet on the forehead.

Their landlord, an old man living all by himself in the decrepit house, took them to a local nursing home in his car. It was a wise decision, because the streets of Delhi were on fire that evening, and they could both have been killed. Over the next two months, they stayed in the nursing home. The landlord paid for their hospital fees.

I sat in the deli, across him, stunned into silence.

"We decided that India was no place for us," Mr Singh said, looking at me. "We left India in March 1985 and arrived in Brampton. We have been here since then, and we have never gone back."

We sat in silence; we had been at the deli for more than an hour. I could see that the memory of that period still lived in him.

"We should be going back," I said.

"No, let us have another cup of coffee," he said. He got up and went to the counter to order. He returned, holding the paper cups.

"I am sorry if I bored you with my story. I haven't had a chance to talk about my past to anyone in a long time," Mr Singh said.

I nodded.

"Did I bore you?"

"Oh, no, no, Mr Singh, not at all."

"Good. I wanted you to know about me."

"But I don't know everything about you. I mean, your story doesn't end in 1985. What about your life in Canada?"

"Oh, that is a different story altogether. I remember when we finally reached Canada, it was such a pleasant surprise—a cleaner, unpolluted country. My first impression of Brampton was that I was in Delhi or some city in Punjab—with all those turbaned men, and women in Indian attire. It was cleaner and smelled better. But that initial delight at finding the familiar in an unfamiliar place was short-lived when I realized quickly that despite being in such an amazingly beautiful place, most Indians continued to remain angry all their lives in Canada," he said.

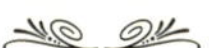

I recalled that Gunjan had told me something similar when she saw my naive excitement at being in Canada. "An immigrant's life gets progressively harder, and that innocent wonder at the beauty of the world that marks the first few years turns into hardened cynicism," Gunjan said in her matter-of-fact tone. "You will develop it too—a permanent scowl."

"Mr Singh, you aren't talking about yourself," I said.

"Oh, I have nothing to hide. We struggled initially. But not for long. Jasmeet completed her bachelor's and then her master's and then her doctorate in political science. She began to teach at the University of Toronto. I started this trading business because I didn't want us both to be in the same vocation."

"You must have grown children," I said.

"Grown grandchildren. My daughter is a banker in Ottawa and my son is an IT consultant in San Diego, both have two children each. Jasmeet took premature retirement and now devotes her time to the Punjabi Community Health Services and does fund-raising for charity in Punjab."

"You should both visit India now," I suggested.

He looked at me, smiled, and said, "Yes, I think we should. But India seems so foreign, so alien now."

Family

After four years at Singh Traders, I was unemployed again because Mr Singh decided to sell his trading company to a Canadian food supply chain. He probably made millions, but I lost my job. He was impersonal about it.

"I want to spend more time at home," he said.

I nodded.

"Let me know if I can be of any help," he said amiably, and patted me on my shoulder as he led me to the main door of the office. "You take care," he said, and waved goodbye, as I walked down the stairs with my belongings in a banker's box.

Gunjan was waiting for me in the parking lot behind the office building. She helped me put the box in the car trunk and we drove home.

I wasn't unhappy about losing the job because I had started earnestly looking for a better-paying position. Even before Mr Singh informed me about my imminent termination, I had been contemplating doing something in journalism or writing.

I had tried the usual channels available to newcomers to find work. I participated in workshops at the local community centre in Bramalea that was supposed to make newcomers job ready. I volunteered at the centre to create marketing flyers for its programs in the hope that it would lead to new contacts and career opportunities. It was futile—only middle-aged couples who lived in the area came to the centre, on Saturday afternoons; all were polite and friendly in an insincere sort of way that I had come to realize was called Canadian politeness.

I met an employment counselor at the community centre, Mary Lou, a young Filipina woman who specialized in finding appropriate employment for newcomers to Canada. She examined my resume minutely and asked me to meet her a week later. Then she recommended that with my experience as a journalist in India, I should retrain myself in a communications program.

Fighting my instincts, I asked Gunjan's opinion. She rejected the idea outright.

"It won't do you any good," she said.

"What do you mean?"

"It will only help you in incurring a large student loan and nothing more. We will have to look for a better job for you. But you should not waste time and money on retraining."

I had come to realize that I was incapable of making friends because I came from a cultural milieu that was alien to most Indo-Canadians. I know this sounds utterly snobbish and elitist, but it is the truth.

I tried freelance journalism and approached a local South Asian newspaper for freelance jigs. I went to see editor Iskander Choudhury of the *South Asian Chronicle,* a free copy of which I had picked up.

"Yaas?" he answered loudly.

I introduced myself and told him briefly what I was looking for.

"We don't need freelancers," he said, again speaking loudly. "We use whatever is published in Pakistani and Indian newspapers. And some local news is done by me."

When I looked at him eagerly, he softened his gaze, nodded, and ran his fingers through his salt-and-pepper beard.

"Look, young man," he said, speaking to me in a heavy accent that firmly placed him in Punjab. "You shouldn't think about this" (he meant journalism). He nodded sagely, all the while running his fingers through his beard. "It is not practical. You won't ever make money."

I called another newspaper—the *South Asian Weekly News*—and spoke to its editor Ramesh Sharma. He called me to meet him at his home office.

"Sharad, you have done serious journalism in India. Here, the standards are different," he said.

"I am just looking for an avenue," I said hesitantly.

"You write if you want. I will publish it. But I can't pay. You write regularly and build a portfolio. That may help you eventually. But I can't pay."

I wasn't keen to write without being paid. However, I was determined to find work in a sphere where I had experience and skill, and so I began to write on a weekly basis for the *South Asian Weekly News*, initially offering editorial commentaries on developments in India and then occasionally reporting on local community events.

It was exciting, initially. I was writing after a long gap, and I was delighted that I hadn't lost touch. I worked on a report on automobile insurance premiums being high in Brampton, and a feature on the role of religion in a multicultural environment. After about four months of writing for free, it became monotonous and boring, and more than anything else, it was the "free" part of the freelance that really bothered me.

All marriages, without exception, eventually turn out to be uneasy compromises, when love turns into responsibility. The transformation begins when a couple becomes parents. In our case, Gunjan was already a parent, and I assumed the role immediately when I saw Arty. So the transition, the compromise, was sooner, much sooner.

Our lives together acquired permanent tension within a couple of years. For me, the main, perhaps the sole reason was Gunjan's inability to let go of her past and forget Frank. She forced herself not to be depressed and tried to involve me in her life, but I was not allowed to pry into her past. She guarded her memories fiercely and even prevented me from asking Arty about Frank.

Her reticence about her past gave rise to guilt and she tried to overcompensate by focusing on making my life comfortable, by constantly being busy with household chores and turning everything I asked for into some sort of directive, an order that had to be filled immediately, no matter what.

When I lost my job at Singh Traders, she went into overdrive to help me find a better alternative. She spoke to her colleagues at work and put the word out among her friends. She even forwarded my resume to Frank, who, I was surprised to learn, was willing to help.

Frank called a friend, one thing led to another, and a certain James Cochrane of Standard Instrumentation and Equipment Inc. called me for an interview. The company was planning to expand and needed someone who could manage external communications and create campaign collaterals.

The office was on the twelfth floor of a multistory building on Yonge Street at Sheppard in Toronto.

When I met him at his office, James looked at me uncertainly.

"We need everything in English," he said.

I nodded.

My nod didn't make him comfortable; he gazed at me with serious misgivings.

"Why don't we do this—you take some information about our instruments and equipment and do a flyer that highlights all the key features," he said.

I nodded again.

"You will have to talk to me for me to better evaluate your abilities," he said, looking at me with exasperation.

"Yes, of course," I said. "I am confident I will be able to do all that you need. I will send you the flyer by tomorrow morning."

I pushed my certificates and recommendations in his direction, and he examined them minutely. I looked around his office. It was a functional workspace without any unnecessary accoutrements. The office staff—the three people who were visible—were of different races. It seemed to me that all Canadian workplaces looked the same.

"Okay, you send me the writeups and if they are any good, I will call you tomorrow," he said, and handed me my certificates. "These don't mean anything to me."

I worked all night on creating what to me was a marketing promotional flyer that described the different instruments that James's company either manufactured or imported, and emailed it to him.

I expected him to respond at once, but when I didn't hear from him for a couple of days, I called him.

"Yes, how are you?" he said, sounding affable.

"I am fine. I called to find out what you thought of my effort," I said, as casually as I could.

"It was good. I found it to be good. Yes," he said, speaking slowly.

"Oh, I am glad you did."

Then, after what seemed like an extended pause, when neither of us said anything, I asked him: "So, what do you think? Will I be able to do this job?"

"Shadar," he said, mispronouncing my name, "I have already appointed a more experienced copywriter for the position."

The rejection rankled more than it should have. Gunjan seemed to have expected it and tried to give a perspective.

"You are trying to get into a field where traditionally employers prefer white men. Canada welcomes immigrants with open arms, but the Canadian establishment is not ready to accept that immigrants can do everything that they do. They are especially unwilling to accept that South Asians can be proficient in the language they consider their own," she said.

I wasn't in the mood to understand the deeper sociological underpinnings of Canadian society and went out for a walk in the ravine on the other side of our apartment building. I had wanted this job desperately.

Nothing seemed to be working, and I had little choice but to live a life of relative penury and doing utterly boring survival work that was devoid of any relevance to my life. But just when things seemed to be spiraling out of control, I got a call one afternoon from James Cochrane.

"Shadar, are you still interested in that position?" he asked, without wasting any time. "If you are, come and meet me tomorrow at twelve noon."

"I will be there," I said, and before I could say anything more, he hung up. The next day I got the job. The professional copywriter he had employed had left the company for a better paying job elsewhere.

On my way back home from my meeting with "James," I wondered at how swiftly things change in our lives. I knew the job would transform mine. Gradually, my life in Canada was changing for the better. Working in an office and doing mundane routines was way better than making sandwiches wearing transparent plastic gloves for minimum wages.

And now, creating marketing brochures was better than pointless paperwork. The job finally gave me an opportunity to use my abilities, although James said that I would also have to get involved in administrative and maintenance tasks.

The company hired me to create marketing collaterals. Then, as it diversified, I was tasked with creating content for its new line of instrumentation products, which was in the realm of technical writing. I was promised that gradually my responsibilities would grow to include supervising the creation of marketing material and advertising in industry journals, and I would promote the company at industry events.

Thanks to Gunjan, who dropped me off in Toronto from Brampton, the commute to my new job was not difficult. James greeted me at the door and led me to a cubicle that would be my workspace for the next few years.

"I want you to start simple—just study our product lines and read the existing material for now," he said. "We can work on the revisions and fresh material in a couple of days."

When I nodded, he threw up his hands and exclaimed, "You are banned from nodding in this office. You will always speak."

I smiled, and nodded again, and then said, "Yes, yes," quickly.

We both smiled. "Come, meet your colleagues," he said, and led me through the corridor to meet the members of the SIEI staff. I hadn't realized that SIEI was a large company. I politely shook hands with Tina, Jake, Ahmed, and about seven or eight others whose names didn't register. Then, he took me to the kitchen and pointed at the coffee machine, the fridge, and the dishwasher. "You use these carefully." He smiled and led me back to my cubicle.

"Now you start working," he said, and began to walk back to his office. "Come to me if you need anything. We will meet in the late afternoon."

I would gather later that James was a hands-on kind of person who preferred to do everything himself and had a tough time delegating. A technocrat, he knew his business and knew how to make money. He needed people to implement his ideas. I read the brochures and studied the designs and made notes.

I had found the verbiage of the brochures replete with jargon. I took two brochures and began to rewrite the content in simpler, more basic language. The content I created left more space for designs. When I showed the revised content to James, he patiently read it and then looked up.

"I have used basic language and less words so that there is more space for design," I offered.

"This still needs work."

"Oh yes, this a draft."

"Good. Let us finalize it before you leave this evening."

I returned to my cubicle and reworked the draft several times. I realized that I would need to quickly acquire some understanding of instrumentation. James had helpfully kept a tome on the subject on my desk. I figured a better way would be to sit with James and understand his business. In the evening meeting I suggested that to him and he invited me for a drink at the tavern on the street below the office. I knew then that I would be working with James for a long time.

Gunjan was excited that I had what she called a "proper job" and was delighted too that Frank had helped me get it.

When Frank came over the next weekend to take Arty with him, it was their marriage anniversary, and it should have been of no consequence, but she hugged him, which she always did, and I felt it lasted longer and was more physical than it needed to be. They were communicating without speaking. They smiled into each other's eyes, which were doing all the talking—Frank's conveyed expiation, apology, and Gunjan's gratitude, acceptance.

At Arty's suggestion, we drove to the Bramalea mall's food court to have Hakka Chinese. John, who owned the outlet, was from Calcutta and spoke fluent Hindi. It seemed he knew everyone in Brampton, everyone who was from or had links to India. At the food court, Frank sat with Arty, and Gunjan and I sat together. But when we got up to pick up our food, Arty said I should sit with her.

Gunjan and Frank liked the idea, but Frank was hesitant and looked at me.

"Oh, it is okay," Gunjan said, and pulled him down beside her.

She put an arm around him and Arty took photos.

John, the owner of the eatery, came and greeted Frank warmly. He smiled at Gunjan, and gave a fortune cookie to Arty.

"You are back in Brampton?" John asked Frank.

"No, just visiting."

"John, I don't think you have met Sharad," Gunjan said.

"No, I haven't. You are Gunjan's brother?"

"Husband, John, husband . . . " Frank said.

"Oh, I am sorry," he said, looking at me, "but it is logical to make such a mistake; you are sitting apart from the family."

I nodded and tried to smile, but couldn't, and my face probably showed my discomfort. John hurriedly returned to his counter.

Frank, Gunjan, and Arty returned to their conversation. The father and daughter were planning to go to New York for the long weekend, and Arty was trying to cajole her mother to go with them. Gunjan saw Frank and I exchange glances and immediately told Arty to stop.

"It is not possible. I have work to do here."

"It is the Victoria Day long weekend, everybody will be out," Arty said, almost in tears.

"It is okay, Arty, it is okay. We will have fun together," Frank said, and hugged his daughter.

But Arty wouldn't give up. She looked at me. "Why can't you be alone for a weekend?" she shouted.

For the first time in a long while, I was angry. I stood up and began to walk to the parking lot. Frank came rushing to me. "Look, I'm sorry, really sorry."

"You don't have to be," I said, calming down, and walking back with him to the food court table. "It's quite alright. She is right. I can be by myself for a weekend."

"I think I will go with them," Gunjan said. Arty clapped in excitement, a smile spreading across her face.

Back in the apartment Gunjan quickly packed some clothes. When the three of them had gone, I saw Arty's fortune cookie on the table and picked it up. The message inside said, "Tell them what you really think. Otherwise, nothing will change."

"Everything changes, everything has changed," I said, and laughed sardonically.

Arty

I had no idea who Ruth Williamson was when I received a call from Brampton Civic Hospital's emergency ward to tell me that she had been rushed to the hospital.

"Who?" I asked, completely at a loss. I was at home, waiting for Gunjan to return from work.

"Ruth Williamson. She says you are her friend Arty's father."

"I am Arty's father, yes, yes. That is correct."

"Could you please come to the hospital as soon as you can. Ruth has slashed her wrist. She was found in the women's room at Bramalea City Centre. She is out of danger but has asked for you."

I called Gunjan at work and told her about the call. She said she would join me there. I called a taxi and soon reached the hospital. A kindly, matronly Punjabi nurse at reception led me to Ruth, who was in a wheelchair, probably sedated and with a heavily bandaged wrist.

"Sharad . . . can I call you Sharad?"

"Yes, of course."

"If you don't let Arty return, we will both kill ourselves."

I was stupefied.

"She will slash her wrist if she is not allowed to return," Ruth declared, gasping with pain. The nurse beckoned for me to keep quiet.

I looked around; people were staring at me. I walked back to the entrance, where Gunjan was waiting for me. I told her about Ruth's warning, and we drove back home in silence.

Gunjan called Frank when we reached home and told him to get Arty back to Brampton immediately.

"Why didn't Ruth ask for her parents?" Gunjan asked Arty when the father-daughter duo reached home.

"They don't know about us."

"And why Sharad?"

"He supported us."

"What is the shortest short story you have heard?"

"Huh?" Arty asked, looking up at me from the game she was playing on her Gameboy.

"The shortest short story?"

"I don't know."

"Well, do you want to know?"

"Not really."

"Arty, what is wrong with you. You are being so rude," Gunjan said.

"No. I am just not in the mood for ghost stories right now."

"It's alright," I said. "She is focused on her game."

"But isn't it our weekly day to tell a ghost story? And it is your turn," Gunjan said.

"It is time we stop this routine. It is well past its sell-by date," Arty said, and walked away to her room.

Arty was now a teenager and had little or no patience, especially with me. I found her discernibly more tolerant of Frank, whom she respected and held in awe.

About a year or so back she had shortened her name, which I thought was already short, to Art. For a brief while she was known as Art Parker. But then she realized that Art was usually a shortened version of Arthur, so she reverted to Arty. Her transformation took both Gunjan and me by surprise; neither of us had even remotely expected this sudden and complete change in Arty's attitude. Frank, too, seemed a bit unsettled by what was happening to his daughter.

She was fourteen years old now and growing into a tall teenager who would become a beautiful young woman in a few years. Her mixed parentage gave her distinct features, and she had the best of her mom and dad. Dull grey in colour, her eyes were almost feline—iridescent, lustrous. Her hair was done in pigtails.

Gunjan took care of Arty's appearance. Her own Indian roots ensured that Arty was modestly yet smartly dressed. But since the previous summer, Arty had stopped wearing the clothes her mother preferred and picked clothes of her choice that I found—to put it mildly—rather radical. I was to learn that her attire was "gothic." One evening she came out of her room wearing black yoga pants that were probably two sizes too small and a black jersey, and a lot of silver jewelry. She had shaded her eyes dark gray and smeared her lips with blood-red lipstick.

I hadn't seen Gunjan's eyes that wide ever before, as she stopped in the middle of a sentence.

"Whoa, what is this? Where do you think you are going wearing that?" she shrieked.

"I am going to Ruth's place. It is her birthday, and everyone will be there. We will go to a movie later."

"What movie?" I asked, before Gunjan could say anything. I didn't want the mother to veto the daughter's evening out merely because she didn't approve of her dress.

"The new Harry Potter movie," Arty said, disdain dripping from her voice, as she flipped back her hair in defiance and stared at her mother.

"And you plan to wear that?"

"We have all decided to wear black," Arty said.

"With your ass hanging out like that?" Gunjan sputtered.

"Mom! I am at least fully covered. Most of the girls are wearing microminis."

"Oh, thank God for that."

"It is okay. Let her wear what she wants," I said, to defuse the tension.

"You don't interfere," Gunjan said curtly.

"Yes, Sharad, it is none of your business," Arty said. "You are not my dad."

We had been here before, on many occasions, so I wasn't shocked, and yet my eyes probably showed my dejection; Gunjan nodded gently at me. I smiled weakly. Arty was talking to Ruth on her cell phone and rushed out.

Arty was a mere child when I met her for the first time. She was all of four years old and cute as a button. But I had been hesitant in building a bond with her. It was my first experience of living with a child. And moreover, I wasn't sure of my role in her life. I wanted her to be close to me but was clueless how to go about achieving that.

Gunjan was keen that her daughter accept me, but to Arty I was her mother's new husband, and not her father. She was friendly, loving, and willingly depended upon me, constantly seeking my approval, but as she grew older, I was more of a friend and clearly not her dad.

"Frank is my dad, Mom," she would say, flatly.

"And so is Sharad," Gunjan would respond.

"Nobody can take Frank's place in Arty's life," I would offer as conciliatory bait to stop them arguing. In Arty's young mind, it was clear—Frank was her dad, and nobody could occupy that space.

She had refused to call me "Dad," and insisted on addressing me by my first name. I found that unusual initially but got used to it. Despite her studied distance and occasional disdain, Arty was well-mannered and affectionate, and like most children, she was not sure how to show her affection.

"It isn't that I don't like you, Sharad. You are the best thing that has happened to us," she often confessed.

Her parents doted on her. Every weekend, she would be with Frank, having started preparing for the visit to Kitchener from Thursday morning, stuffing her knapsack with everything she possibly could. He drove by to pick her up from school on Friday and they returned Sunday evening.

I tried different ways to get closer to her, to make her feel at ease with me, but it always felt forced. I offered to help her with her homework. She agreed reluctantly but stopped after a couple of sessions.

"Your accent," she said, "I don't get your accent."

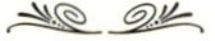

It isn't difficult to get used to Canada's severe cold, but it is impossible to adapt to the clock going back in the winter and it getting dark at four-thirty in the afternoon. I have yet to figure out why this is done, and I suspect no one really knows or has a logical reason for it. One cold December evening, we sat together in the living room, sipping hot chocolate.

"It is only half past five in the evening and it is already as dark as inside a chimney," I said.

"How do you know? Have been inside a chimney?" Arty asked, as always in a mocking tone.

"No, I haven't even been in a house that has a fireplace," I said. "But I would imagine that it couldn't be darker inside a chimney."

I asked her whether she believed in ghosts. She was on her Christmas break from school, getting ready to be with Frank.

"No."

"Do you want me to tell you a ghost story?"

"There are no ghosts," she asserted.

"I have seen a ghost."

"Oh, come on, Sharad. I am no longer a child," she said.

"Ignore her. Go ahead and tell us all about it," Gunjan said.

And then, for the next hour or so, I told them of my encounter with Arthur Birkenshaw. They listened with rapt attention; when the story was over, I looked at Arty.

"So, what do you think?"

"It can't be true. You must have been led to believe it was a ghost."

But Gunjan was thrilled. And it was agreed that the three of us would spend one evening a week narrating a ghost story.

That winter was one of the best periods that we had as a family. Every Thursday evening, we would sit in the living room and be together for about an hour, narrating a ghost story. But they didn't know of any ghost stories, so it became my responsibility to narrate a new story each week.

One day I noticed that Arty had a notebook and pencil and was jotting down points.

"I am planning to submit a ghost story as my project for my writing class," she said.

"You should have your own story instead of just regurgitating what you have heard," Gunjan said.

"I am sure Arty can write a ghost story," I said, to encourage her.

The following week, Arty was ready with two ghost stories for her assignment. But she would, of course, first show it to Frank.

Corrine and Philippe at the school

Corrine, a girl in grade 5, was kept in detention by her teacher and made to sit in the detention room all by herself. She fell asleep and when she woke up school was over, and everyone had gone home. She got up and opened the door of the detention room and walked out into the corridor.

"Is anybody here . . . ?" she whispered and then shouted, but nobody responded.

Corrine was scared and began to cry. She tried to open the door of the school's office, but it was locked. She walked in the empty corridors and thought of her parents, her brother. They would all be worried.

She was moving aimlessly through the corridors and stopped to drink water at the water fountain. As she was drinking water, she felt someone tap her shoulder. Surprised and scared, Corrine turned around and saw a young girl.

"Who are you?" Corrine asked.

"I'm Philippe," the girl answered.

"What are you doing here?" Corrine asked.

"Oh, I'm trapped here," Philippe answered.

"What about you?" Philippe asked Corrine.

"I have been locked in here. Will you help me get out of here?"

"I don't know how," Philippe replied. "I have been here for so long and I don't know how to get out."

"What do you mean?" Corrine asked. "You have been here long? How can that be? You could have left in the morning."

"I can't come out in the morning . . . " Philippe answered. Corrine found that strange. But she was keen to get out, so she asked Philippe to help her push a bench from the classroom to the telephone just near the school's main door, and together, they pushed a wooden bench to the telephone.

Corrine dialed 911 and gave all the information about herself and Philippe to the police. The police arrived in ten minutes and broke open the main door from outside. Corrine was rescued and taken home, and in all the excitement she forgot about Philippe.

Her parents were relieved when she was brought home. When the commotion had subsided a bit, and Corrine was alone with her parents, she asked her mother, "Did they take Philippe home?"

"Who is Philippe?" her mother asked.

"She was also inside the school with me. She helped me push the bench to the phone so that I could call the police."

Corrine's mother immediately called the police and informed them about Philippe. The police rushed another patrol to the school, which was now open, and informed the principal and teachers about Philippe.

They looked for Philippe everywhere, but couldn't find her anywhere. The school's administration checked all their records of students but couldn't find anyone named Philippe. Intrigued by this, the police searched their missing persons records and found that a Philippe Balland had been reported missing in 1959 from the school and had never been found. Her family had moved to Quebec soon after her disappearance and the case was closed.

Arty changed her school when she reached high school because she wanted to specialize in computer science. It was probably her mixed genes that made her into something of a genius. She had a natural talent in subjects that most kids would have found difficult, such as math. Her grades were consistently high. Then, a year or so into high school, things changed.

For the first time, her grades began to slide and she didn't seem to care. Her outlook on life and on herself changed almost overnight. She began to devote a lot of attention and time to her appearance, clothes, shoes, and bags, and complained incessantly about her hair.

Gunjan agreed to most of her daughter's demands, even when she didn't have the resources—financial and emotional—to fulfil them. She was the ever-accommodating single parent, who constantly sought approval for raising her only child.

After two semesters of low grades, Frank suggested that perhaps it would be better if Arty moved with him to Kitchener. Gunjan seemed to like the idea, but Arty wasn't sure at all.

"All my friends are here."

"And they seem to be the problem," Gunjan said.

"Mom, you just don't get it, do you?"

"I think I do. I don't want you to ruin your life."

"How the fu . . . how am I doing that?"

"By hanging around with your retarded friends."

"Mom, you are a racist."

Frank, who was quietly listening to this exchange, finally intervened. "Okay, let us do this—you stay here with your mother and make sure your grades improve. If they don't, then we move you to a high school in Kitchener for the last two years."

"But Dad, that is not fair."

"You work hard and do better and you can be where you want to be," Frank said, in a tone of finality that ended the conversation.

The situation didn't improve for Arty and her grades stagnated. She became desperate. And she started to talk to me, especially when Gunjan was not around.

"You have to help me, Sharad."

"Yes, let us start working on your weakest subjects starting today."

"No, that is not what I mean."

"Then?"

"Tell Mom that moving me to Kitchener won't do me any good."

I could sense that Arty wanted to say more but was hesitating. I turned off the TV and focused on her.

"Sit and tell me what is going on in your life. You say I am not your Dad, and I have begun to accept that. But we have always been friends, so you can trust me."

Arty looked at me for a while and then abruptly came and sat on the couch.

"Sharad, I am in love with a girl."

I looked at her and didn't say anything. My silence compelled her to keep talking.

"Ruth and I are in love. I can't leave her and go to Kitchener. That will kill her, and me, too . . . " She looked at me earnestly, and then began to sob when she saw utter incomprehension on my face. I had no clue what I was expected to say.

"Arty, I think you are too young to make such life-altering decisions," I said, though my voice must have sounded uncertain.

"Yes, I know. You are right. But I can't help how I feel," she said.

I wanted to help her but wasn't sure what to do. I didn't want her to do anything rash, and at the same time I couldn't stop thinking what could have triggered her to seek and find same-sex love, and why she was confessing to me. All I knew was that she was too young to know her mind, to know what was good for her, or to know anything at all about life.

"Let me think about this," I said.

"Sharad, there is nothing to think about."

"No," I said as forcefully as I could. "There is actually a lot to think about. The first thing that comes to my mind is that you must be separated from your friend for some time so that you can assess your feelings about her. And for that reason alone, you should move in with Frank in Kitchener."

"That doesn't make any sense to me. You are finding it hard to accept that I am a lesbian."

"You are fourteen. You will feel differently in six months, and then again in a year or two. This is the age of transition. Nothing about you that you think is permanent is so, everything will change, and will keep changing when you become an adult."

"This isn't helping me at all," she said.

"You take time to think about all this and I will do so too. Let's work together to find a solution," I said in a bid to find some time to work out something that would be acceptable to everyone.

She walked up to me and showed me a photo of Ruth and her together. To my surprise, Ruth turned out to be a black girl. My astonishment must have been evident on my face, because Arty giggled.

"What? You expected a white person?"

"Actually, quite frankly, yes," I said with a laugh.

"You are so Indian, so racist," she said. "Talk to Mom, Sharad. Please talk to her. I don't want to go to Kitchener."

"Arty, do you want me to tell her about Ruth and you? Believe you me, if she knows about that, there is no way she will let you be here even for a day. And your Dad's reaction won't be any different."

Arty didn't wait for me to tell her mother about Ruth. To my surprise, Gunjan was not as disturbed as I expected. Her concern was focused on Arty's grades. She called Frank and told him about

Arty and Ruth, but the phone conversation was relaxed. Neither seemed inclined to treat the matter seriously. I was wrong.

"She is fourteen," Gunjan said. "At her age, sexuality and sexual identity is new and raw. It is exploratory, I guess." She was giving words to her emotions, saying things aloud to convince herself that eventually everything would work out fine.

"Frank is coming to meet me tomorrow morning, but he is not coming here," she added, looking at me but quickly averting her gaze and looking down at her hands. Her brows were knitted tightly together. "I have failed as a mother. I am sure Frank is convinced of it," she said.

"I don't think you should take such a drastic view," I said, and walked up to her to hold her hand. "It isn't the end of the world. You must persuade her to go to Kitchener."

She pushed me away probably without realizing what she was doing. The next day, Gunjan met Frank for lunch. That evening, she looked relaxed. They had worked out a solution—both Arty and Gunjan would go to Kitchener. Gunjan would accompany her daughter and be with her for a week or so to make her relocation bearable and help her get adjusted.

I wasn't sure this was a good solution but didn't say anything. If it helped Arty, I wouldn't mind being alone.

Gunjan returned after a week, leaving Arty behind with Frank.

But Arty rushed back upon learning that Ruth had slashed her wrist and was in hospital. There was no other option, Arty remained in Brampton.

Rape

Gunjan wasn't willing to talk about us, about her past, about Frank, except repeatedly playing the victim card and declaring that he had walked out of her life when she "caught him cheating." But it wasn't only about her past and Frank. She would clamp down on anything that could even remotely be termed as personal. Her refusal to share her past left me searching for meaning in our relationship. Her tendency to freeze up after giving me a glimpse of the fierce wildfire that periodically destroyed her mind made me feel like an unwanted guest in her life.

Gunjan overcompensated for her reticence by constantly trying to please me and look after my needs. She was energetic, attentive and meticulous in anything she did—from cooking to cleaning to laundry to getting groceries, and she insisted on doing everything herself. She made notes of what I liked, what I didn't like.

Gunjan was raised in a rich family. Coming to Canada was a culture shock for her, and she confessed it had taken some years for her to adjust to her new reality. But there is a distinction between being self-reliant and being independent.

In one of her rare moments of candour about her life with

Frank, she confided that it was only after Frank left her that she had learnt to do the basic household chores.

"I cooked, and Frank took care of the house," she said.

"So, what went wrong?"

"I don't know, maybe it was because I wasn't a good cook. I couldn't cook his food," she said, then she looked at me forlornly. "Perhaps that is why he went to Cynthia's home for dinner. It began with once a week, then three days, and then almost every evening." And then she looked away. I walked up to her to hold her, but she brushed me away.

This had been a rare moment when she let me inside her world, her past, but she wasn't comfortable with me being in it for long, so she shut me out again.

"I probably have OCD," she often said.

"Let me help you in some household chores."

"You come from a labour surplus economy, where you have helpers for everything. You aren't used to doing household chores," she said.

"I can learn. I want to help you."

"There are other ways to help."

That usually ended our argument because I wasn't likely to earn more than her or even as much as her anytime soon.

"Life is tough here. Get used to Canada," she often said.

After a decade of maintaining the home and earning for it, I could see that she was on the verge of a breakdown. And she was turning resentful, and the resentment began to manifest in small ways.

One Sunday morning, soon after I had started working at Standard Instrumentation and Equipment Inc., I pulled Gunjan away from the kitchen and brought her to our bed.

"I am happy with you, I am fine here in Canada, what is making you so insecure about us?"

"What do you mean? I know you are happy here. I am making sure that you are happy," she said.

"It is not about you making me happy, Gunjan," I said, unable to conceal my annoyance.

"Sharad, my relationship with Frank failed because he felt I was too focused on my career and wasn't doing enough at home. I am not going to let that happen again," she said, her voice a mixture of remorse and apprehension.

I held her close and tried to kiss her, but she pushed me aside.

"I have to make breakfast for us, and then I have to run down to get the laundry done before the washers are full in the laundry room, and then I have to get lunch ready," she said, and got up.

"And then you have to get groceries and make supper, iron clothes, help Arty with her homework," I said.

"No, she is going home. I mean, Frank's coming to take her," she said, and then looked at me and was about to say something but hesitated.

"Gunjan, let me help you," I said, fighting my urge to say that even after all these years, she didn't feel at home with me, but instead I said, "Let us divide the chores."

"No, no, you are not used to this kind of work," she said.

"But you are going crazy with all this work."

She walked away from the bedroom and went to the kitchen. I followed her and tried to help her by doing the dishes, but she wouldn't let me.

"Sharad, don't do this. We will make love in the afternoon," she said.

"It is not that," I said, my voice rising. "We need to talk about things that are creating this rift."

"There is no rift!" she said, almost shrieking. "All you want to talk about is my past with Frank, but I am not interested. It is over."

I glared at her and walked out of the kitchen.

While she was unwilling to talk about anything that involved us, Gunjan spoke all the time about her work at the pathology laboratory and about her colleagues. It made for animated conversations, and it was fun. She encouraged me to talk about my work and about my boss, but there wasn't anything that I could think of.

I didn't argue with her because I didn't want to hurt her. She continued to be dutiful, driving herself to exhaustion. Invariably, she would fall asleep while we watched TV, and then she would walk to bed in a stupor and snore away till it was time to get up and start the day.

One night in bed I woke up feeling her hand inside my pyjamas. It was still pitch dark. I groaned when I saw the clock beside the bed. It was 2:17 AM. I was in no condition to do anything but sleep.

"Go to sleep," I whispered, and pushed her away.

She began to sob loudly, and I reached out to her, but she pushed me away.

"You are cruel."

I tried to wipe away her tears, but only managed to poke her eye. She stifled a scream and her sobbing intensified. I moved from her and turned away.

Unable to sleep now, I got up from bed and made my way to the kitchen. I pulled out a bottle of whiskey and poured myself a drink. The clock on the oven showed it was nearly three in the morning. The light from the street partly lit up the kitchen and the living room.

Alcohol burnt my innards as it flowed down my throat; it soothed my nerves. I had no idea what to do with our situation. Gunjan needed a break, and we could easily have taken a vacation if we didn't have to save up to buy a home. Her brother Suresh had hinted that he would pay for our vacation, but both Gunjan and I had recoiled at the idea of someone else paying for us.

Loneliness and alcohol are a lethal combination that easily led to depression. I wondered whether Gunjan and I had ever been in love, could ever be in love. I wondered whether this had been a marriage of convenience for her, and for me. She was utterly dutiful to all her responsibilities, but I always detected an absence of the spontaneity that was so palpably evident in her interactions with Frank. Yes, there was affection, but it seemed to me that for her, our marriage was no more than a duty.

About an hour later I returned to the bedroom. Gunjan never used a blanket. The light from the street highlighted her curves. In a stupor, I sat beside her on the edge of the bed and put my hand on her waist. She stirred in her sleep. Overcome with desire, I took off my clothes and slid beside her. She mumbled but continued to sleep.

I began to pull down her pyjamas and was mildly surprised at how easily I could pull them all the way down. I quickly mounted her and pushed myself inside her before she could do anything. She woke up with a start and tried to push me away. She let out an audible gasp. She freed her hand from my grip and slapped me when I tried to kiss her.

She was breathing heavily. I tried to kiss her again and she slapped me again. She could have screamed but didn't and after a while, she stopped struggling. When it was over, she turned away. I could hear her sobbing before I dozed off.

It was almost dawn when I woke up and went to the kitchen. I had left the whiskey bottle on the dining table. I poured another drink and gulped it down. When I returned to the bedroom, I saw her lying on the bed, her pyjamas still coiled at her feet. I couldn't stop myself and again turned her around. She sat up and pushed me away.

"Sharad, stop it. You are raping me; Arty will get up," she whispered.

"I need you," I murmured.

"No, you don't need me. You just want to fuck. Anyone would do."

Gunjan pushed me away, got up from the bed, and went to the kitchen. I dozed off again.

By the time I woke up, it was midmorning. Mother and daughter had left. Gunjan had left a note on the dining table. It said, "It is all over. I want you to leave." The note was beneath the empty bottle of whiskey.

I was groggy and called my workplace to inform them that I would be absent that day. I made tea. It cleared the fog from my mind and it dawned on me that while in a drunken stupor I had raped her. With every passing moment, my remorse grew. I called Gunjan, and surprisingly, she immediately answered. Normally, she wouldn't. Her workplace had strict rules about receiving calls.

"I am sorry."

"Sharad, it is over."

"I am coming to your lab. I need to talk to you in person."

"It won't change anything."

And it didn't.

In the week following that ghastly night, she mellowed but was determined that we couldn't live together any longer. She had sent

Arty away to Frank's place for the Christmas break. When Arty hugged me as she was leaving with Frank, I felt the embrace was a bit tighter and lingered a bit longer. She smiled as I patted her head and ran to Frank, who was waiting for her in his car.

I wanted to save our marriage, but Gunjan was looking for a break. We agreed to a mutual separation for two years. We agreed to meet every six months to assess our feelings.

We never got back together.

Faith

I met Jane at an industry exhibition, where my company was exhibiting its latest range of ultraviolet spectroscopes. The exhibition was at the Mississauga Convention Centre and Jane had been assigned to assist me.

"Hello, I am Jane from Paramount Exhibitions. Hope you have got everything you need," she said, standing outside the booth. I had been late reaching the venue and visitors had already started arriving.

I nodded and smiled.

She was wearing a business suit—black trousers, white shirt, a bright yellow jacket; and what I remembered forever—bright magenta shoes. She quickly set up the booth—installing the rollup banners, starting the A/V loop from my laptop, and setting up the catalogue display. Meanwhile I engaged the visitors. Later I noticed that Jane had sat down on one of the two chairs inside the booth.

I nodded and smiled again.

"Is that all that you do? Nod and smile. I know you are Sharat because I saw your profile on the website in the exhibitors' section," she said, and laughed.

"Sharad . . . the name is Sharad, ends with a *d* not a *t*," I said, and broke into an embarrassed laugh. "And thank you for helping me. You saw what a mess I was. The exhibition starts too early."

"Yeah, but most visitors prefer to be here early and then go to work," she said. "Do you want me to get coffee for you?"

"No, not right now. I will have tea a little later," I said.

After about an hour, the crowds began to thin. I looked around and noticed that all the booths had a couple of attendants, mostly young women probably doing part-time work to make some extra money.

"Some of them are here every year," Jane said, pointing the coffee mug she was holding at the booth across the aisle, then immediately put her hand down. "I shouldn't be pointing at anyone," she said self-consciously.

I looked at the women she was pointing at, and then at Jane. She had a wide, sincere smile. Her black eyes sparkled and became wider as she talked, her hands waving animatedly. Her hair, also black and parted on the side, fell easily on her shoulders. She was tall, and her magenta shoes made her look taller.

"What does your name mean in your language?" she asked, looking at me in an earnest sort of way.

"It means fall."

"Fall? Really, you have such names?"

"No, no, I mean the season, autumn, not to fall down," I said with a laugh.

"Oh, yes, that makes sense," she said, and smiled, embarrassed.

At lunch, she opened her bag and pulled out a sandwich, a banana, and a bottle of apple juice. She looked at my lunchbox and politely said, "That looks interesting," and then quickly looked away. I had been in Canada long enough to know that when people find something "interesting," they are just being polite.

It dawned upon me that although she looked every bit an Indian, she wasn't. I had met such people in Toronto, and I had learned that the easiest way to identify them was by their accent. If they spoke without an accent, even though they were of Indian origin, they were no longer Indian in any sense. I had also learned that people didn't like to be asked where they were from. I couldn't understand why that was such a big deal. For some reason it was considered offensive, especially by people who were non-white immigrants. When asked, "Where are you from?" they would testily reply, "I am Canadian." Just to rile them a bit, if I had asked the question I would say, "I am a Canadian, too, but I am from India."

I was hesitant asking her, but was equally keen to know, and so after a brief and inconclusive debate with myself, I asked her, "Where are you from?"

"From Scarborough," she said, and smiled, but her tone gave her away; she was playing with me.

"I am from Brampton."

"I thought you were from India," she said, and laughed.

"I thought you were from India, too," I said.

"No. I am not from India," she said.

"So where are you from?" I asked.

"I am born and raised here. My mom is a Canadian, her great-grandfather was a farmer in the Steppes in Russia, and her grandfather and father lived on a farm in Newfoundland, and my dad came from Guyana. They met at McGill and lived in Scarborough after they graduated."

"You look Indian . . . South Asian."

"I guess when you mix a white human with a black human, you get a brown human," she said, then she flipped her hair and giggled self-consciously.

"But Guyanese are brown, aren't they? They were originally all from India."

"That's what my dad says too, but not to my mom; to her, he's always been black."

Over the next few weeks, Jane ruled my mind. I hadn't thought of anyone or anything else except her. I couldn't focus on work or even cook meals at home. Home was now a rented apartment on Keele and Lawrence West. I was done with Gunjan and Arty and Frank, and wanted desperately to move on.

Although I was lonely when I met Jane, I wasn't looking for a relationship. I was in my mid-fifties, but she was a welcome distraction. She was young, energetic, talkative, pleasantly attractive. When I couldn't stop myself from thinking about her all the time, and when the thoughts became overbearing, I gathered enough courage to call her. The recording at her phone extension informed me that she was at another show. Hesitantly, I left a message saying I had just thought about her and felt like saying hello, and also wanted to thank her. Then, feeling acutely embarrassed, I wrote a long-winded email, giving her unnecessary and irrelevant details about how amazing the show had turned out to be, and that my company had secured two orders from it.

She replied to the email almost immediately and gave me her cellphone number. "Call me after work."

I waited impatiently for five PM, but not wanting to sound too eager or seem desperate, I called her about an hour after reaching home. She didn't answer, and again, I left a message with my name and number. I wasn't sure she would call back.

I was desperate to talk to her.

She called late that evening.

"Hi, Autumn," she said; she sounded tired.

"How are you? It has been a while," I said, trying hard not to sound excited. She remembered the meaning of my name, which definitely meant she remembered our day together.

"Yes, indeed, it has been a long time. I was hoping you would call me. I didn't because I wasn't sure you would be free to talk," she said.

"You have returned from some exhibition?" I asked, changing the subject to quell my excitement.

"Yes, this one was on e-commerce; actually, quite interesting."

"What are you doing this weekend?" I said.

"I will be at my parents'. I have to take my dad to the cardiologist," she said.

We agreed to meet in a couple of weeks. But almost immediately began to text each other. Some relationships develop unhurriedly from initial diffidence to growing comfort. Even if we didn't meet as often as I would have wanted to, it didn't matter. Jane loved movies and we went to a multiplex once to see *Star Wars*. She was a fan. She also loved experimenting with different cuisines.

For the next three months we went for dinner and movies every Friday evening. At the end of the evening, I would drop her off at her apartment. We didn't kiss, we didn't even hold hands. I wasn't sure of her age. She seemed to be in her late thirties.

"We won't go out this Friday evening," she said. "You come over, we will watch a movie, order takeout."

That evening, after watching television and after a feast of naked burritos, we made love at her apartment. It was unhurried, natural. She hugged me and kissed me on my eyes. I held her lightly and fell asleep.

Our routine changed, and I was at her apartment every weekend. After about six months, she told me that she had spoken to her parents about me.

"They want to meet you," she said.

"Of course, I would be happy to meet them," I said. "By the way, I am fifty-five years old."

"Oh, okay. I am forty-two. My parents have a condo on St Clair and Jane; we can go together next Saturday."

There was a thirteen-year gap between us. It wasn't much, or so I convinced myself as we left her apartment together on Saturday morning to meet Samuel and Alexandra Wilson—Sam and Sasha. They turned out to be much younger than I had thought, and from what I had seen in the photograph Jane had showed me.

"Welcome, Sharad," Sam said, shaking my hand lightly. Sasha hugged me. I sat on the couch between Jane and Sasha, and Sam sat on a large, comfortable leather armchair. I noticed their clothes were an odd mix of formal and casual; both looked uncomfortable in them. I was quite certain that Jane had made them wear these clothes; she had forced me to wear my formal clothes, which I had to iron that morning. After some time—during which time we spoke briefly about my job, the weather, and the recent dismal Leafs game, about which I knew nothing—we exhausted all topics of conversation and sat in silence.

To break the awkward silence, Jane turned to me and said, "My mom works as an accountant in a downtown office." Sam looked at me and forced a smile but didn't say anything.

"We will have lunch at noon; that is okay, right?" Sasha announced, and got up.

"Let me help you," Jane said, and followed her to the kitchen.

It was a ploy to get Sam and me to talk alone. I wasn't ready for it, and from what I could see, neither was he.

I drummed on my knees tentatively and looked around the living room. It was small and neat. There was one large window and next to it was a bar with a large selection of wine. A distinct aroma of cooked meat filled the room.

"Jane tells me you are from Guyana," I said to Sam, making a desperate attempt to sound natural.

"Yes, I came here four decades ago, when I was young. I have been here longer than I was in Guyana," he said, and then got up to pour himself a glass of wine. "You may pour yourself a glass if you want," he said, looking at me.

I nodded. "Maybe later," I said. He shrugged in response and took a large sip from his glass.

"When did your forefathers come to Guyana?" I asked, to start a conversation.

"I have no clue, maybe a hundred years ago, maybe even more, along with all the other slaves, I guess," he said, looking at me in genuine surprise. "Why? Does it matter?"

"Oh no no, not at all," I said, and then looked at him. "They were not slaves surely; they were indentured labourers."

"Oh no, they were all slaves, have no doubt about that. That bit about indentured labour is colonial fiction," he said.

I lapsed into silence and began to drum the armrest again, this time slightly more vigorously.

"You are into marketing," Sam said. It was evident that this wasn't the question he wanted to ask.

"Well, it is a job like any other. I do whatever I am expected and required to do, but yes, a lot of what I do could well be classified as marketing," I said, and even as I was speaking, I realized that my answer was long-winded.

"Sharad, both Sasha and I have thought about Jane and you, and we don't know what will come out of this relationship, but what we can see is that Jane hasn't been this serious with anyone in a long time. After Alex dumped her and married someone else, that was six years ago, Jane has been heartbroken and has refused to be in a relationship. So, we are happy as her parents that you are the reason she has nursed herself back out of depression." Sam spoke fast, as though to get over with whatever he wanted to say.

"She has told us about your marriage, and how it ended," he added, and looked at me intently.

I nodded, not sure whether I was expected to say anything, but definitely not keen to have a chat with a near-total stranger about how my marriage to Gunjan had failed.

Now it was Sam's turn to lapse into silence. He fidgeted, gulped down his wine, and got up to refill the glass.

"Want one?" he asked me.

"No, thanks."

Sam filled his glass and looked at me. He stood by the bar, surveying the room, and then he began to hum a tune. With nothing to say or do, he looked at me again and said, "Give me a minute, I will see what they are doing. It is mealtime." He called out to Sasha.

"Just a minute!" she hollered back from the kitchen.

"I will be right back," he said, and headed for the kitchen.

Jane came and led me to the dining table. The spread on the table was elaborate. Her parents stood beside it, beaming. "We have a Canadian menu for lunch," Sasha said. "A combination of recipes from Newfoundland, the Caribbean, and some bit of India."

I nodded.

"Mother has cooked Jiggs dinner, a Newfoundland specialty. It is corned beef, turkey leg, mashed potatoes, stuffing, cooked greens, and boiled cabbage," Jane said, as she served me. It smelled delicious. "Father helped us make the Guyanese Metemgee."

"I generally make it with meat, but have made it with saltfish today, because we already have the Jiggs dinner," Sam said.

"And Jane made the Indian-style chickpeas—the chana masala."

"This is too much . . . " I mumbled, "it must have taken all day . . . "

"All of yesterday and today," Jane said.

"Yes," Sasha said, and smiled in satisfaction. "I hope you like it."

I nodded.

Before we began, Sam led the family in praying. "Bless us, O Lord! for these Thy gifts, which we are about to receive from Thy bounty, through Christ our Lord. Amen." I sat in silence looking at them. Jane looked at me and smiled.

During the meal, as I focused on the food, the family discussed health matters. Sam's heart condition was stable. Sasha had recently started a physical routine at home and had once again modified her diet to control her diabetes. I realized that her parents depended upon Jane for everything—right from making medical appointments to paying the maintenance for the condo, and paying for their everyday expenses. She kept an indulgent eye on me, keenly observing me as I tried the different things that she served. I marveled at Jane's sense of responsibility, her budgetary skills, and her affectionate disposition.

The family prayed again after the meal. Then, before we got up, Sam asked Jane to get the gift. She had kept a gift-wrapped package on a chair beside her. She handed it to Sam, who, rather ceremoniously, gave it to me.

"I don't know whether you like reading. But even if you don't, you will love this book for its originality."

I looked at him and nodded.

"Open it and see," Sasha said.

I carefully unwrapped the package. It was a book, Saint Augustine's *Confessions*. I had never heard of Saint Augustine. My incomprehension was evident on my face.

"Saint Augustine is one of the greatest thinkers known to mankind," Sam said, "And *Confessions* is one of the greatest works of Western literature. I am sure you will find it interesting."

"What is it about?" I asked.

Before Sam could say anything, Sasha said, "It is his autobiography and is about his conversion to Christianity."

We returned to Jane's place by taxi.

"So, what do you think?" Jane asked back in her apartment.

"About what?"

"My parents."

"They are nice."

"That is it? Nothing else?"

"No. I mean there was a bit of awkwardness in our interaction, but that was natural because we were meeting for the first time," I said, and then, after a pause, emphasized, "but they were polite."

"Yes, and they liked you, too."

"Oh, what did they say?"

"That they liked you," she said, and smiled.

Then she went to change and I opened the book that her parents had given me.

Grant me Lord to know and understand which comes first—to call upon you or to praise you, and whether knowing you precedes calling upon you . . .

Jane came in and sat beside me. She looked at me and then at the book, and waited for me to speak.

"Why did they gift me this book?" I asked. It seemed like a natural question, and she was expecting it and ready with an answer.

"Otto, they want you to become a Christian, a Catholic, before we get married."

My jaw dropped. I gaped at her. She looked at me and then

she held my hand, and pulled my head to her chest. I got up from the couch, unsure of what I should make of this suggestion. I mean, changing religion, and converting from one to another wasn't something that I had factored into the relationship and how it would progress. Yes, I definitely wanted to marry Jane and from what I could see, she wanted to marry me. But becoming a Catholic was not in the plan at all. I spent the weekend thinking about it and nothing else. I mean, I had never been a religious person. I wasn't an atheist or some such thing, but religion had never been central to my existence. I didn't pray every day or go to the temple regularly. I didn't know much about my religion. But for the fact that I was a Hindu because I was born into Hinduism, there wasn't much that I knew that would classify me as a Hindu. I knew some *shlokas* because I had heard my Dadi chant them during her elaborate pooja. I knew of some of the gods because I had seen their photos or *murtis* that Dadi worshipped. But there was a gap of decades between what I had seen and distractedly observed from my Dadi's devotion. Gunjan was a devout practitioner and performed the pooja every morning, but her pooja wasn't as elaborate as Dadi's, and it was all done quietly.

I had to choose between religion and love, and it was clear to me that I valued love more than religion at this stage of my life. I was unlikely to find anyone remotely like Jane. The choice, therefore, was easy. I would choose love. And I said so to her. Jane was overjoyed, and immediately called her mother to let her know. I interjected and told her to inform her dad too; which she did, squealing in enthusiasm. It appeared to me that both of them—the parents—were happy with my decision.

Dadi

"She died last night," Neeta said, her voice calm and emotionless.

"Why didn't you call me then?" I asked.

"Bal and I were busy making the arrangements," she said. "It was too much work."

I couldn't say anything as Neeta described the funeral.

Since I came to Canada, I had anticipated this moment—Neeta calling me from India to inform me of Dadi's passing. I had always imagined I would be devastated by the news, that I would break down and cry. But I didn't. Jane's presence in my life had changed me, brought calmness and certainty. Time had passed, I had left India a while back, and Dadi's looming presence in my life had long receded.

Neeta had called when it was morning in Bombay, late evening in Toronto. As I heard Neeta's voice, I was lost in thoughts. Memories of Dadi came flooding into my mind. Wrinkles had lined her face, and they multiplied a million times when she frowned or smiled. She wore thick glasses that made her small eyes look large. Her widowhood had banished colour from her life, and she wore only white. She had been a widow for four decades and more and now she was dead. But one memory predominated: the smell of cooking and prayers. She exuded an odor—a mixture of wheat flour, incense sticks, pooja flowers, and sandalwood.

Dadi was diminutive physically but had been a looming presence in our lives. She rarely smiled, didn't talk much, and often dripped sarcasm when she did. She stoically went about doing her chores and lived in our kitchen where she prayed and cooked. The small kitchen seemed smaller because of its heavy furniture—a wooden storage shelf for groceries, with a small shrine on a side.

On the phone, I heard Neeta's sniffle. She told me Dadi had worried about me after I moved to Canada. "When I think of her," Neeta said, "I realize how similar we both are to her. She never consciously taught us anything. We just absorbed everything that we saw in her."

"Do you want me to come to Bombay?" I asked, hoping she would say no, and she did.

"No, it's okay. Bal has handled everything quite well." After a brief pause, she said, "We are selling the building. Sadanand Kaka's son is buying it."

"That's a good decision," I said.

"We will keep your share here in a fixed deposit. You can use it when you come here or arrange to get it transferred to Canada," she said.

"Sure. That's fine."

There wasn't much else to say, so after a few minutes we disconnected, promising to call each other more frequently.

A million memories crowded my mind that evening as I thought of my grandmother. But two remain etched in there. Many years ago, one of Dadi's cousins died in an accident. I took her to meet the family. The autorickshaw broke down and we had to walk a long way. The walk turned out to be an ordeal for her.

"Dadi, you have come here to console the family, so you won't talk about your walk," I told her.

She was too tired to say anything. We sat with the family for a while, and then returned home. A few months later when the daughter of that cousin came visiting, Dadi recounted the harrowing walk to her.

"Why didn't you tell us then?" she asked.

"Sharad instructed me not to. He thinks about others. *Dukhi thava no chhe*. He will suffer."

It is perhaps the best compliment I have ever received.

Another time I caught her in a pensive mood, sitting by the window, watching the traffic on the road.

"You are lonely," I said.

"*Ekla rehvani tev chhe*. I am used to being alone," she said.

That sentence has also stayed with me. Staying alone—it is the one thing that we are not prepared for, and inevitably we have to learn it the hard way.

Only once had I seen her resolve to keep her own counsel break. That was when my mother's health deteriorated rapidly. Ma had begun to disconnect with the world and lapse into inconsolable and ceaseless weeping. She wouldn't get out of her bed, and would mutter curses at her long-dead husband, my father. At such moments, I often heard the name "Aparna" uttered with venom. Even after she was moved to the sanitarium, she continued to have these bouts of extreme anger and weeping.

"Why can't she just forget that Aparna?" I asked Dadi in exasperation.

In a rare moment, Dadi shouted at me, "That *randi* ruined our family!" then stopped herself in horror, cupping her mouth with her hand, a look of pain in her eyes. We were in a state transport bus returning from Khandala to Bombay and she looked around quickly to see if she had been overheard.

"I am sorry," she said, "but promise me you will never repeat that word ever." She held me tight in her arms.

"It's okay, Dadi, I won't. But Ma must move on in life, she keeps whispering that name in anger, and then she turns abusive."

"She is a wreck because of my son," Dadi muttered. "Nothing I do for her will absolve me of my sin."

"But Dadi, you were not responsible. There must have been a reason or many reasons," I said, consoling her. "Also, it is time all of us just move on in our lives. Baba has been dead for a long time, and Ma has been in the sanitarium for a long time also."

The decision to move Ma to a sanitarium in Khandala was tough on all of us, and especially Dadi. But she was practical. Ma's physical health had deteriorated, too. She had acute rheumatoid arthritis, which confined her to a bed. She had also developed Alzheimer's. Dadi had spoken to Sadanand Kaka's son, who was a successful businessman in Poona, and was now buying the tenement from Neeta. He knew a trustee at the sanitarium. "It wouldn't cost us much," Dadi muttered when I said that it would probably be better if we just kept Ma with us. "Keeping her here will be more expensive emotionally on all of us," she said in a tone that discouraged any discussion on the subject.

I remember the day the ambulance arrived in front of our building. Dadi told Neeta and me to hug Ma, which we did, but she didn't hug us back. She smelled of urine. And her eyes seemed lifeless. She didn't protest as she was carried out of the house by a burly attendant from the sanitarium. "Be gentle with her," Dadi said sternly to him.

Initially, Dadi went to the sanitarium every month to check on

Ma. On her return, she would sit with us and tell us about her condition. Ma seemed to be progressing well. Both Neeta and I hoped that she would return soon. Then, gradually, the frequency dropped to once every quarter; and she took me with her. When I saw Ma on my first visit to the sanitarium, I realized immediately that she would never return. She didn't recognize us, and when a stern nurse ordered her to look at us, she obeyed her, and after a fleeting glance, looked away. When Dadi tried to speak to her, she began to whimper, and the nurse requested us to leave the room, as our presence was disturbing Ma.

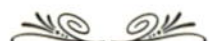

A few days after Neeta's call, on an impulse I decided to go to India. I wanted to see Ma and was apprehensive that I wouldn't be able to meet her at least once before she died. Neeta immediately approved of my suggestion. She sounded excited.

"Yes, you come over. We will stay at a hotel in Bombay and we now have a bungalow in Khandala," she said.

I wanted Jane to accompany me. She had never been to India, and this would be a great opportunity to know the place, especially Bombay. But she was not interested.

"You go. You must go. It will be cathartic," she said.

Neeta and Bal were at the new airport in Bombay to receive me. They had come in their own vehicle—a swanky, electric-blue Japanese SUV hybrid manufactured in India. Neeta was smiling through tears. She was wearing a white shirt, beige jacket, and matching cotton trousers; I had never seen her in such an outfit before. Bal was attired in business casuals; he had gone bald, but looked fit. He was sweating profusely.

We settled in the car. Bal asked Dinesh to turn the air-conditioner on full blast. He wiped the sweat off his brow with a handkerchief. I found it strange that a handkerchief was still being used. I had stopped using it in Canada.

I was returning to my hometown after two decades. It was a different place, but it still smelled the same—a combination of rotting garbage in open sewers and exhaust fumes. I had not imagined there would be so many vehicles of all shapes and sizes clogging the narrow roads.

Neeta told me of their ready-made garment business. Bal had started it in Surat and was now exporting to Europe and the United States. Neeta assisted him. They had become the archetypal entrepreneurial couple, India's new rich. I politely asked them about their three daughters.

"The eldest, Saroja, is in London, the second, Vivekta, is in Delhi, and the third, Rucha, is here in Bombay. All busy with their careers; all married, but we aren't grandparents yet," Neeta said. She smiled broadly, nodded vigorously.

They had reserved a suite for me at the Grand Imperial Hotel in Teli Gali. In all these years, I had never actually stayed in the hotel, or even had food at its restaurant. Kishore and Radhika were there to receive us, as were Monali and Jagan. Neeta had planned a grand yet personal welcome for me in Bombay.

From Monali I learned that Abdul had moved to Canada even before me and that his son, Rafiq, had become a "terrorist."

The next morning, we started for Khandala, to the sanitarium where Ma was staying. I asked Neeta about the expenses, and she said Bal had been paying for Ma's stay for over two decades. I wondered about Dadi's assessment of Bal. She hadn't been totally fair. I couldn't think of anyone better for Neeta. I looked at him; he, too, was beaming with pride. I nodded at both and smiled. It felt good to be back with my sister.

We reached Khandala soon—a new expressway now connected

Bombay to Poona. It was better than anything I had seen in Canada. We were to be at Bal's new bungalow at the edge of the valley that was appropriately named Valley's Edge. I was beginning to comprehend the extent of Bal's prosperity. From the large balcony of his second floor, the view was stunning. The valley was covered in monsoon clouds, and the visibility was barely a few metres; we could hear the roar of a waterfall in the distance, and the cacophony of birds happy to be in the wild. Periodically the cloud cover would disappear to reveal a deep gorge.

Bal had bought the bungalow in Khandala to provide an alternative home for Ma. The ground floor had been turned into a makeshift nursing home. Ma was at the sanitarium when I arrived, and an ambulance brought her to the bungalow. I was surprised to see Ma getting down on her own, though accompanied by two attendants. We went down to receive her.

"Ma, this is Sharad," Neeta said. "You remember him?"

Ma looked at me hesitantly as the attendants helped her into a wheelchair and lifted her up the front stairs. We quickly settled on the chairs on the verandah. Ma continued to gaze at me intently. I wasn't sure she recognized me. But a few moments later, her eyes glistened with tears, she raised her hand to her mouth to stifle a sob. I got up from my chair and hugged her. She went limp in my arms and then gave a scream—a loud, guttural shriek.

Bal said to the attendants, "Take her inside to her room,"

"Is she able to speak at all?" I asked Neeta as we followed inside. She nodded and said, "Sometimes."

I couldn't remember when I had last heard Ma speak.

Neeta had brought a few old photographs of the four of us taken at Marine Drive, near the flyover. She pointed at me in the photo and then at me beside her and said to Ma, "This is Sharad."

"Sadashiv . . . Premeela . . . " Ma mumbled.

Neeta clapped her hands and hugged Ma. Except on that one occasion, Ma didn't speak at all during the week we spent together in Khandala. But she gave enough hints that she remembered me. She seemed healthier than before, although years of living at the sanitarium had obviously taken a toll. Within a week of my return to Toronto, Ma passed away.

I had taken Abdul's telephone number from Monali and called him. He was pleasantly surprised. We met at a Tim Horton's in Mississauga, where he had a home. Abdul had aged, but was as forthright as before, and spoke about his son's traumatic mental health problems that had almost made him go over to the "other" side. Fortunately, he had held on to a sense of right and wrong, Abdul said. I told him about my failed first marriage and my marriage to Jane. "I am now a Catholic," I said. He seemed puzzled. "Religion only causes misery," he said with a smile.

Afterword

A writer lives forever in his published words. This posthumous publication of Mayank Bhatt's novel in linked stories is an event of celebration and joy. We are fortunate for it to come out, three years after the author's untimely passing from cancer.

Mayank immigrated to Toronto from Bombay (Mumbai) in 2008, but he said that India was always close to his heart. He wrote about the experience of being an immigrant, and an emigrant, in both his nonfictional and fictional works. He wrote a column in *Canadian Immigrant* magazine, and worked as Executive Director of the Indo-Canadian Chamber of Commerce until the last day of his life, July 31, 2022. Mayank's wife, Mahrukh Pasha Bhatt, has described how, ill though he was, he sent his last work emails on July 31. He died on August 1st. Mayank's work ethic and perseverance are part of the reason this book is here today.

I met Mayank in 2010 on the memorable occasion of our both being published in an anthology. We shared interests in literature, as well as the experience of being immigrants to Toronto, and became friends. Mayank completed three writing mentorships, two of them at the Humber School for Writers, during which he worked on his first novel. He immersed himself in Toronto's writing community. He was an outgoing person, charming and kind. He attended book launches and literary events, participated in readings and festivals, and unfailingly read, reviewed, and promoted the work of his fellow writers. He cofounded and curated a vibrant reading series which continues to this day, bringing writers and their work together, and to the public. Mayank was the best kind of literary citizen, whose generosity, friendship, and loyalty will long be remembered by the community.

Conversations about literature (or about history, or world affairs, or politics) with Mayank were illuminating and wide-ranging, often surprising, and revealing of his sharp intellect. His background in India, after all, had been in journalism. And so Mayank was also the best kind of global citizen: informed, curious, passionate about Canada as well as India, and committed to communicating his thoughts the way he knew best, by writing.

In the years after the 2016 publication of his debut novel, *Belief*, Mayank was writing the stories that constitute this book. He steadfastly continued writing, even when he became ill. Mahrukh attests that he continued writing and doing research for his stories to the end of his life, in the same way as he continued supporting his friends' works, until the end. My debut novel was published three months before Mayank's death, when he was very ill, but he purchased the novel, read it with careful and rigorous attention, and told me what he thought about it. He was working and thinking until the end.

Mahrukh tells us that Mayank had intended this work to have twenty stories, but the cancer stopped him finally, and this book consists of only fifteen. We are left to contemplate the final stories and the books Mayank might have written, had he not left us, too young and too soon. Most certainly, he had more to write: more ideas he wanted to explore, more stories to imagine.

Mayank the storyteller is the protagonist, really, of this collection. These stories delicately, plainly, and fluently trace the social worlds of postcolonial India, and Toronto through the eyes of a newcomer. They tell of forbidden marriages across social and religious divides, arranged marriages, and even attempted arranged marriages. They trace lives of love, conflict, family, poverty, and work. They are stories about human lives and human consciousness, which is the terrain, of course, of all storytellers. The beautiful and evocative cover of this book is a photograph of Bombay (Mumbai) at night: vibrant, huge, and overwhelming—Mayank's hometown.

The achievement of this publication is owed to Mayank's devoted and beloved wife, Mahrukh, to the faithfulness and work of his editor MG Vassanji, and to his publisher Nurjehan Aziz of Mawenzi House. How grateful I feel to these three people.

Through the existence of *Trachea and Other Stories*, Mayank's intellect, imagination, and joie de vivre are again alive and with us. They communicate to us his ideas, their particular terrain, and their magic.

Dawn Promislow

MAYANK BHATT immigrated to Toronto in 2008 from Mumbai (Bombay). Since then he was actively engaged with the Toronto literary scene and was a board member of the Toronto Festival of Literature and the Arts (FSALA). His debut novel, *Belief*, was published by Mawenzi House in 2016. His short stories have been published in *TOK 5: Writing the New Toronto*, *Canadian Voices II*, the *Maple Tree Literary Supplement*, and the *Beacon*.